My Foe Outstre
Beneath the Tree

Also by V C Clinton Baddeley in the Dr R V Davie series

Deaths Bright Dart
Only a Matter of Time
No Case for the Police
To Study a Long Silence

Other titles in the Cambridge Crime series

Douglas G Browne 'The May Week Murder'
Aceituna Griffin 'The Punt Murder'
R E Swartwout 'The Boat Race Murder'
VC Clinton Baddeley 'Death's Bright Dart'

My Foe Outstretched Beneath the Tree

BY
V. C. Clinton-Baddeley

Ostara Publishing

First Published by Victor Gollanz Ltd 1968

Copyright [c] The Estate of V C Clinton Baddeley

ISBN 978 1906288 04 4

A CIP reference is available from the British Library

Printed and Bound in the United Kingdom

Published by   Ostara Publishing
                      13 King Coel Road
                      Lexden
                      Colchester
                      CO3 9AG

The Publishers would like to thank Mark Goullet, Richard Reynolds, and Christine Simpson for their assistance in the reprinting of this book.

Dedication

For Mary and John

In the morning glad I see
My foe outstretch'd beneath the tree.

William Blake

1

I

Miss Eggar steered the estate car past the rhododendrons and drew up before an elaborate Victorian mansion.

"Welcome to St. Martha's," she said.

Dr. Davie maneuvered himself out of the car and looked up at the house. Embossed on the keystone of the porch a stag's head peeped roguishly at him from an encircling collar. Underneath was the date 1871. On the surrounding lawns were splendid cedars. In mild patches of gold, daffodils shone in the declining sun. Beneath distant hedges lay little cliffs of yesterday's snow.

"You will observe," said Miss Eggar, "that it really is red brick."

"This jibe about the red-brick university has always bewildered me," said Davie. "My college at Cambridge is red brick. So is St. John's. So is Trinity great gate. Half Cambridge is red brick. What's the matter with red brick?"

"It depends," said Miss Eggar, "on the brick."

"Well—yes. But the snipe who invented the label didn't know that. He clearly thought that the best universities were built of marble."

"Am I to understand that they are not?" said Miss Eggar.

Davie laughed. He had taken a fancy to Miss Eggar ever since reading her botany book *Poisonous Plants*—for Miss Eggar had wit: she had illuminated a botanical catalogue with curious details about the classic achievements of the great poisoners.

"Come in," said Miss Eggar, mounting the steps and pushing open the door. "I'll show you your room. It's only one flight and an easy one."

"How very pleasant!" said Davie. "A late example of what used to be called port wine stairs. A broad step and a shallow rise. Just the thing for after dinner."

"Our founder and benefactor, Jethro Tonks, was greatly interested—so I have been told—in his creature comforts," said Miss Eggar. "I confess I am rather given to port myself."

"So am I," said Davie.

"Good. We will have some this evening. Now this is you." Miss Eggar opened the first door in a yellow-carpeted corridor. "It looks across the back lawn to the new buildings, which, far from being red brick, are made entirely of glass and concrete."

"So I dimly perceive," said Davie. "This isn't a red-brick university at all. I have been imposed upon."

"Bathroom next door. Come down when you are ready and we'll have tea. The door on the left as you reach the hall."

So Davie unpacked his small case, put out his shaving things in their appointed order, and laid his lecture notes on top of the dressing table. Then he washed his hands, peered at himself in the glass, combed his hair, and examined the books on his bedside table—which proved to be a heavy biography of Dame Margaret Dunstable, eminent meddler in other people's business over a period of fifty-seven masterful years; a new book of poems by Stephen Mossop; and Annabel Champion's latest country house mystery, *Who's for Murder?*, its glossy jacket displaying a hypodermic syringe mysteriously couched upon a dish of peaches.

From the wrapper of the big biography Dame Margaret fixed him with a critical and expectant eye. Almost in duty bound he opened the book and glanced at chapter one.

"Margaret Dunstable," he read, "was born on May 29, 1872, at the vicarage, Spewsbury, the ninth daughter and the fourteenth child of the Reverend Arthur Dunstable and his wife Henrietta, daughter of Captain Custance of Chipping Sodbury. She came from a long line of clergymen and officers on both sides of her family, and it was doubtless from these sources that she drew those high ideals of service which were to mark her out even as a child . . ."

"Goodness!" said Davie under his breath. He laid Dame Margaret down gently and picked up Miss Champion.

" 'There must be some explanation for the disappearance of the cucumber,' said Miss Murchiston."

So it was a Miss Murchiston book. Davie preferred Miss Murchiston to Chief Inspector Banbridge. Miss Murchiston solved her cases by instinct—which was unfair but preferable to all that boring expertise about police procedures. Davie didn't care a damn for the police: he liked doing the detection himself. "There must be some explanation for the disappearance of the cucumber." Davie shut the book firmly. He did not want to be late for tea. But how important, how enormously important, opening paragraphs were, he was thinking, as he closed his bedroom door and set off along the yellow carpet in quest of the drawing-room and Miss Eggar.

The lights were on in the passage. As Davie reached the landing a young woman crossed the hall. She was small and stepped so lightly that she made no noise at all. He waited, watching her as she paused outside the door on the left of the stairs, her hand on the knob, as though suffering from some nervous complex about entering rooms. Then she opened the door, revealing lamplight on the lacquered side of a gold and black tallboy, and a corner of pink carpet; and "Come in, Mary," said the voice of Miss Eggar. "Dr. Davie will be down in a minute." Someone to do with the Poetry Society, thought Davie, deciding automatically to dawdle. He had been given a minute and he would use it.

There were water-colours of Florence and Capri and Taormina on the staircase wall. He stayed to look at them, reminded of pictures painted by his great-aunts at the end of the last century. Nothing would ever look as bright, as pretty, and as peaceful as this again. But Aunt May and Aunt Sophy had both died out there of typhoid fever. So who had the better of it? An ancient question without an answer: though in his heart he thought that probably they had. To have arrived in Venice in a boat with tomato-red sails: that would have been worth a risk.

On an oak chest opposite the foot of the stairs a great bowl of daffo-dils and catkins stood reflected in a long looking glass. Davie observed himself waist-high in flowers. It is a common and erroneous belief that vain persons foolishly suppose themselves good to look upon. On the contrary, vain people are only making the best of what they humbly con-sider an unsatisfactory job. Davie was not deluded. But he liked to do what he could with himself, even at his age. Once again he adjusted his tie. Then he opened the drawing-room door.

At the far end of a long room a log fire blazed on a Victorian-Baronial hearth. To the right of the fire Miss Eggar was seated at a table, pouring out tea from a large melon-shaped teapot. On the sofa opposite the fire the young woman was sitting. On the hearth rug in various attitudes of abandoned pleasure lay four cats.

"There you are, Dr. Davie," said Miss Eggar, "and here is Miss Cragg, who runs our English Department."

Miss Cragg was small and dark and shy, but she had an engaging smile, and Davie noted with approval that she said "How d'you do?" without any of that "Very well thank you" nonsense. No one up to 1930 had ever treated "How d'you do?" as a question requiring an answer, or rather the correct answer was to say "How d'you do?" back again. But nowadays people seemed to think they ought to supply a bulletin. He knew how it had happened: the words that used to be murmured with formality were nowadays screamed and italicized. "My dear! How *are* you?" was the way they did it now, and it is very difficult to say "How d'you do?" in reply to that. Davie usually said "In a rapid decline" or "Not much better," which was apt to fling the stranger off balance.

"You take that armchair," said Miss Eggar. So Davie sat down on the other side of the fire, and Miss Cragg passed him the buttered toast and a cup of tea in which he detected the flavour of red bergamot. Admirable Miss Eggar! Naturally a botanist would know about red bergamot, but how many would bother to use it?

Miss Eggar proceeded to introduce the cats.

"The one who is stretching, and I have no doubt intends to sit on your lap at the earliest opportunity, is Reginald," said Miss Eggar. "He is gay— in the modish sense of the word. He never takes the smallest notice of women, but the moment a gentleman appears there is a great rubbing of head against the trouser leg, followed, if no rebuff is offered, by a carefully planned leap on to the knee. You have been warned. The yellow one with the pink nose—"

"Precisely the colour of the best cut of salmon—"

"—is Harold. He is called Harold because of his snooty expression. After Mr. Macmillan originally, but the name is still appropriate. The white one is Dora. The tabby had to have rather a grand name to compensate for—"

"Yes, yes," said Davie hastily. He did not want the tabby to be offended.

"His name is Xerxes."

"And are they all related?"

"Intimately. Harold and Dora are brother and sister. Reginald is Dora's son. Xerxes is the grandson of Dora's mother, Maud, who passed on some years ago. His mother, Maud's daughter Fanny, Dora's half-sister, made a rather poor match with a tabby from a neighbouring garden. She disappeared one day and left us little Xerxes."

"And a very splendid cat he is," said Davie.

Xerxes gave him a long stare and lifted his left leg behind his ear in the posture of one playing the cello.

"I brought them all down from the north," said Miss Eggar, "when

I came to St. Martha's last September. So far they have made no criticisms."

Miss Eggar poured out more tea. "Miss Cragg makes our English course," she said.

"Tell me about it," said Davie. "Why 'makes'?"

"The Principal means that I direct the tape."

Davie looked blank.

"It's a recording. We make this English course on tape. It's designed by Dr. Marchant."

"You've heard of him, Dr. Davie?" said Miss Eggar.

"Certainly, and know him slightly. He belongs to my club."

"Dr. Marchant gives us a script illustrating different stages in English conversational grammar, and we record it down here."

"You have your own studio?"

"Yes, and then we make copies of the tape and send them out to subscribers—mostly in Europe, but some of them go to Japan and South America."

Davie felt a soft head against his leg. Reginald, who had approached the new gentleman's chair as though by accident, was indulging in exploratory advances.

"If you don't like cats, Dr. Davie, don't hesitate to tell him," said Miss Eggar.

"I couldn't possibly do that."

"Well, just make it difficult for him."

"We have plenty of women's voices to choose from," said Miss Cragg. "And if we want a man we hire an actor. The idea is to give them grammatical constructions and pronunciation at the same time."

"Pronunciation?" said Davie. "Nowadays the air hums with pronunciations which would have been quite wrong twenty years ago."

"Hasn't that always been so?" said Miss Eggar.

"Yes, of course it has. Smart Victorian ladies talked about 'cawfee'. Today cont*roversy* is becoming contro*versy* before our very ears. Cont*roversy* used to be so dreadfully wrong. In another twenty years I suppose it will be correct. Now that the vast majority of people can positively read they pronounce words according to the evidence of their eyes."

"Have some of this very superior cake," said Miss Cragg.

"Thank you—but do go on talking: I'm interested."

"You regret that?" said Miss Eggar.

"Deeply. But Fashion and Tradition are continually at war, and Fashion always wins. Resist Fashion and you're an old fuddyduddy."

"Sometimes a thing tries to be fashionable and fails," said Miss Cragg.

"Certainly—like the *Daily Mail* hat, and the Edwardian clothes which were taken up by the wrong people: it fails and therefore is not fashionable—or it is not fashionable and therefore it fails."

"Like unsuccessful treason," said Miss Eggar. "By the way there's a fashionable word going about that I don't at all understand. 'Camp.' Some silly woman told me the dining-room curtains were camp—the ones with the cupids flying about and all those fauns. When I asked her what she meant she said '*You know*', which is the most irritating of all present day verbal incompetences. And of course I don't know, nor I think did she."

"I wouldn't bother to find out," said Davie. "The word had a meaning twenty years ago. For a coterie it had an exact and entertaining meaning (though from what derived, Lord knows). Then it was taken up by the gigglers and the despoilers, who used it for everything. Today the word means nothing at all. It's been run to death and can't ever be revived. But not before it had been translated across the Channel. I am told it is all the rage in Paris to say things are 'très. camp'. I'm not sure how they pronounce it: and I don't know what meaning they attach to it. Something like their own, and now antique, 'chi-chi', I suppose. People who use the word 'camp' are usually a bit camp themselves."

"But what *was* the original meaning of 'camp,' Dr. Davie?" said Miss Cragg.

"Well—let me see. A calculated extravagance, a kind of archness, a scarcely perceptible wink, a public display of a private understanding—oh, a sort of secret masonic sauce-box."

"It sounds like a poem by Gerard Manley Hopkins," said Miss Eggar. "And I don't think it is at all a fair description of the dining-room curtains. I would have thought the behaviour of Reginald was perhaps a little camp. What do you say, Dr. Davie? And it's no good attempting to create a diversion, Reginald, by jumping on Dr. Davie's knee, because it's time we gathered ourselves together. Dinner is at a quarter to seven, Dr. Davie, and then we'll go across to the small library."

"I forgot to ask—is there a lectern?"

"Yes, there is."

"I'm so glad. I was once given a violin stand. One needs to be very short to be able to make use of that. And they collapse at dramatic moments."

"Did yours?" asked Miss Cragg.

"It did. Everyone enjoyed it very much."

II

The small library was a pleasant oak panelled room which had been created by the late Jethro Tonks for his own especial relaxation in the company of his own collection of unusual books. Half of these had lived on the open shelves and were there to this day. The other half—the more unusual of the unusual collection—had been kept locked away in glass-fronted bookcases. These books were no longer in the library of St. Martha's. Indeed it had been the original intention of Harriet Tonks, relict of the above, to burn the lot: but on the earnest representations of her solicitor, and of a gentleman from Bloomsbury, who, within the bounds of decency, had taken the earliest opportunity after the funeral of calling on her, she had been dissuaded from following her first determination, had sold the entire collection for a large sum and had devoted the proceeds to the foundation of several handsome scholarships for the daughters of the indigent clergy.

It was a Harriet Tonks scholar—one Daphne Maiden, daughter of the vicar of Spenlow-in-the-Water, Norfolk, and totally ignorant of the source of her benefaction—who proposed a vote of thanks to Dr. Davie for his kindness in visiting the Poetry Society and for the interesting lecture which they had just heard on "Irony in Poetry". It would, said Daphne, be remembered for a very long time; and would be a source of inspiration to them all.

"Oh, dear," said Davie to himself, "I do hope not. That would be disastrous."

And then Miss Eggar was saying that they would return to the Principal's Lodge where some of the committee had been invited for coffee and light refreshments. "I hope it won't be an awful bore, Dr. Davie."

"Not in the least."

"It is very good for them to have an opportunity of meeting people. They will ask a lot of questions."

"Of course. So they should. I shall be delighted."

"Miss Cragg will be there and one or two members of the staff."

The staff had mostly been sitting in front at the lecture and Davie had been aware of their graver faces against the merrier ones a little farther back. One in particular had seemed to be irresistibly in his line of vision—perhaps because she attracted him by physical repulsion. Davie had many pet dislikes: the plucked eyebrow, the painted cupid's bow which fails to conceal the thin cruel lip of a rapacious strumpet, the dark parting which betrays the truth about a head of golden hair. That especially gave him the willies. This lady, undoubtedly handsome, notably well-dressed, exhibited all those marks of Jezebel. She also wore long adhesive talons obscenely varnished ebony. No one could have failed to notice her anywhere. No one was intended to fail to notice her. Indeed, Davie was pretty sure he *had* noticed her somewhere, in circumstances quite different from these.

She was the first person to arrive at the Lodge, and "Let me introduce you to Dr. Marie Baendels," said Miss Eggar. "Dr. Baendels directs our biology department. She used to be in films. Forgive me." And Miss Eggar moved across to some girls who were standing at the doorway's brink, fearing to launch away.

"Films?" said Davie. "Gracious! Were you starring?"

"No," said Dr. Baendels with a throaty laugh. "I certainly was not."

The laughter released a gale of warm scent from somewhere in Dr. Baendels's corsage.

"Then you must have been 'co-starring'," said Davie, "or 'also starring' or perhaps 'guest starring'—that covers everyone nowadays, I think, except for 'With' and a few in small print who come under the heading 'And'. Everyone is some sort of a star in the film world. It is a most comforting thing and proves beyond any question the high level of talent which these productions are able to enlist—wouldn't you agree?"

"As a conversational opening, yes—but you see I wasn't an actress. I worked on the making of the film. Editing. And it wasn't that sort of film either. They were educational."

"Ah!" said Davie, "I see it all. Starring Bacteria, co-starring Streptococcus, guest starring—"

"You have it precisely," said Dr. Baendels.

"What does 'editing' mean in films? I am colossally ignorant."

"It's snipping out the bits you don't want and joining up the bits you do want in the order you want them."

"I remember those fascinating pictures one used to see of a flower bursting into bloom. One doesn't see them nowadays. I suppose they're old-fashioned—but it was the same idea, I take it."

14

"Exactly. If you'd had the whole process you'd have been there all night. An editor selects."

"Here is the secretary of our Poetry Society," said Miss Eggar. "Daphne Maiden. You heard her speak just now."

"Yes, indeed," said Davie. "Thank you for your kind words."

Daphne was serious and determined.

"I wanted to ask you, Dr. Davie—how does one *know* when a poem is irony? I mean what is the principal characteristic?"

"Why—a straight face, I think. Sarcasm is a cad. He pretends to disguise his meaning but he certainly never intends to be misunderstood. Satire does not even pretend. But Irony is bland as milk. The person who creates an irony affects an ignorance of what he is doing. He works so gracefully that the person who, in a manner of speaking, is being ironed out, is hardly aware of the fact. It is the third party who sees the point."

"Oh . . ." said Daphne.

"Have a sausage roll," said Miss Eggar. "And let me introduce Caroline Mostyn-Humphries."

"There's a young man of that name in my college," said Davie. "Or was. I don't know if the authorities have got rid of him. He was a pleasant chap, but he would climb over the college walls instead of using the normal approaches."

"He's my cousin," said Caroline. "I think he's fab."

"Walls had a fascination for Mostyn-Humphries," said Davie. "It certainly suggests a determination to surmount difficulties. Though possibly not difficulties of scholarship."

The room was full now and Davie moved around answering questions, and talking. The pretty child who asked the inevitable "Who is your favourite poet?" said her name was Lalage.

"I suppose you are going to tell me that you are descended from the young lady to whom Horace addressed his charming verses," said Davie. " 'Lalagen amabo'."

"I don't think so," said Lalage. "I will ask my father. What did you say she was called?"

"Just Lalage," said Davie.

"Dr. Davie," said Miss Eggar, "Miss Cragg would like to show you the studio. Have you time tomorrow after breakfast, before you go?"

"Yes, indeed I have. I would like to see it very much."

"We can show you how we edit a tape," said Miss Cragg.

In a far corner of the room Daphne Maiden was saying, "The person who in a manner of speaking is being ironed out," and several girls beside her laughed. "But you have to keep a straight face," said Daphne.

"I must be going, Principal," said Dr. Baendels. "It has been a lovely party. Thank you for asking me. Good night, Dr. Davie. I enjoyed your lecture."

"Thank you for coming," said Davie.

Dr. Baendels moved towards the door trailing scented clouds. It occurred to Davie that she would have stayed longer if there had been some more men. Himself, he was enjoying the party. It was pleasant at the age of seventy to be treated kindly by a bevy of young ladies. And what a pretty word that was, he was thinking as he went up the port wine stairs half an hour later. A term of venery, a noun of assembly for roes and larks and quails—and by association, for ladies. Modern nouns of assembly were usually lost in the sandy wilderness of facetious humour. "A conspiracy of lawyers," indeed! Our ancestors were more honourably exact. There was truth, onomatopoeic or otherwise, in a gaggle of geese and a pride of lions. Nor was there anything whimsical about a charm of linnets. Charm came from Carmen, a song. Lord knows what bevy came from—but it was pretty. A bevy of larks. A bevy of roes. And, by association, a bevy of young ladies.

Davie got into bed, plumped up his pillows and reached for a book.

"There must be some explanation for the disappearance of the cucumber," he began.

III

At about the time that Dr. Davie was rising to address the ladies of St. Martha's on the subject of Irony in Poetry, Morris Brent opened the door of the Ristorante Torcello in Dean Street, Soho. He had booked the small table in the corner by the window.

He was alone. Morris Brent liked dining alone. It was cheaper. And he could have a better dinner. On the infrequent occasions when, for some reason of strategy, he did entertain an acquaintance, he would go somewhere less expensive than the Torcello. And that would be for lunch not dinner. He had also developed a useful technique for such occasions which kept the order within bounds. Guests usually take some time studying the menu: they like to be given a lead. Brent was always quick to give it to them. He named one of the cheaper dishes as being exactly what he wanted, and when the waiter asked what they would have to follow he would say, "Just coffee for me—how about you? There are some good things on the trolley, I believe, if you like that sort of thing," and the guest invariably replied that coffee was just what he would like too.

But when he was alone Morris Brent could sometimes afford to go to a better restaurant. And that was what he was doing this evening. The Torcello was a very good restaurant indeed. He glanced at his watch. He had an hour and a half. Without the interruptions of a business conversation, that, he thought, was a reasonable time for a leisurely dinner.

The waiter brought him a menu in area about the size of *The Illustrated London News*. After studying it very seriously for five minutes he ordered *melone con prosciutto*, duckling, orange salad, and asparagus (very early and really rather expensive). Afterwards he intended to have a zabaglione, a confection of which he was inordinately fond. It was extraordinary how many restaurants, well knowing how to make it, yet failed to achieve total perfection. A zabaglione must have the proper amount of marsala in it—and it must *be* marsala and not some muck conveying the marsala flavour. Be mean about that and the thing was ruined. A zabaglione must be the same all through. Be mean with your trouble and you got a little puddle at the bottom. A zabaglione must be hot. In so many restaurants it arrived not much more than warm. It was just a matter of taking trouble and not being economic about it. "The mark of a bad zabaglione," Morris Brent would say, "is meanness—just that. It's an expensive dish both in skill and in ingredients. If it's not made properly it's not worth having."

He also ordered half a bottle of excellent claret. And a glass of sherry to go on with.

It was, after all, a special evening. Never the time and the place and the loved one all together. That might reflect the experience of the late Robert Browning. But at nine-thirty that evening it was not going to be true for Morris Brent.

For a few seconds he thought affectionately of Lucy. But sherry reminded him of the dining room and the long mahogany table at which his grandparents had always done themselves so well, though strangely devoting the rest of their lives to proving with chapter and verse that the world was in the clay feet period of Nebuchadnezzar's dream and would shortly be destroyed, a disaster (the infant Morris was given to understand) not many people (even in another world) were expected to survive, with the exception of Mr. and Mrs. James Multravers, their immediate family, and a few of their friends. Mr. and Mrs. Multravers had in fact been summoned to their account before the expected cataclysm had taken place and had left it to their daughter to continue the propagation of their theological discoveries.

Maud Brent had not had as great a genius for interpreting the prophets as her father had had, but she had piously published his book and had done her best to frighten her husband, John Brent, and when he was carried off by a consumption at the age of thirty, she had not disguised her belief that such was the reward of a misspent life. There had been darts and she did not know what else. She had determined that Morris should not follow in his father's deplorable footsteps, and the little boy had been brought up strictly—strictly, that is, in the doctrines of old Mr. Multravers, which although concentrating with relentless attention on the hidden, but to him divinely revealed, meanings of the prophet Daniel, had also demanded the consolations of a well-kept home. Mr. Multravers could find authority for everything he did. "Wine that maketh glad the heart of man," he would quote: "and oil to make him a cheerful countenance, and bread to strengthen man's heart," explaining that "bread" was not to be taken literally, but that it covered all the kindly fruits of the earth, such as pineapples or peaches, and indeed could be taken to include a sirloin of beef or the best end of a neck of lamb. He would also quote with great effect the marriage at Cana of Galilee.

Maud Brent had had high hopes of Morris. But he had been a clever boy and this had been his undoing. Accepting the indulgent side of his grandfather's theology he had unaccountably declined its serious complement, and before the age of fourteen had not only ratted on the prophet Daniel but had even rejected his grandfather's interpretation of the plagues of Egypt and all his elaborate mathematical deductions from the measurements and proportions of the pyramids. Maud Brent had been greatly grieved but she always maintained that what she called "the real Morris" was sound at heart.

With a reverential flourish a youthful waiter laid the *melone con prosciutto* before him. Morris Brent smiled—first at the melon, and then at his memories.

He had been lucky all the way. When he and that ass Phillipson had tried out the protection racket on the younger boys it had been Phillipson who had been bunked. Morris had been able to persuade the headmaster

18

to give him another chance. Another chance to do better was presumably the interpretation the headmaster had intended. For Morris it had meant another chance to handle his amusements more successfully. And he had done so. In spite of the fact that he was a born bully, Morris had always succeeded in being popular. He was exceedingly good-looking.

The wine waiter brought the claret and poured out the regulation mouthful. Morris waved his hand genially. "I'm sure it's all right," he said. He had long ago decided that the ceremony was absurd. If the wine was a disaster he could complain, but he found no pleasure in pretending to an Olympian judgment which he knew he had not got. The waiter bowed and filled the glass.

Then the war—bringing trouble for some. He had lost good friends and was sorry. But for Morris himself the war had brought good fortune. To begin with he had made several pleasant acquaintances with gentlemen, which had been much to his financial advantage. He had never been fool enough to press his necessities past a point, but he had done very well. And he was not at all ashamed of his professional record. He had been a good soldier. He had seen fighting. He had been slightly wounded, and he had ended up as a sergeant. He had been well known for knocking hell out of recruits. At which point the memory of a stammering Welsh boy made him smile so widely that the youthful waiter, who was just approaching with the duckling, was enchanted by what he took to be an exceptionally amiable acknowledgement of his services: and perhaps even more.

The walls of the Ristorante Torcello are panelled with crude paintings of that strange island, divided by narrower strips of looking glass. Glancing across the room Morris Brent caught sight of himself between the Byzantine cathedral and a view of the Venetian lagoon. He moved his head to catch as near a sight as possible of his profile. His neck was thicker than it had been twenty years ago, but he still thought, even at forty-seven, that he was the best-looking man he had ever seen. And to do him justice this was an opinion widely held among women. Lucy Werner thought him as beautiful as an archangel though she knew very well that the right sort of archangel had hair of burnished gold. Morris Brent's hair was black as the raven's wing. It was that that made his bright blue eyes so devastating, and it was those eyes that had enslaved all the people he had bullied, from the fags at school to the men he met in the business world which he now inhabited.

"Yes, indeed," said Morris Brent to the proprietor of the Torcello, "everything has been splendid, thank you very much. Particularly that stunning orange sauce."

Arnoldo beamed and enquired what Morris would like to follow. Morris ordered his zabaglione. It would have been better to order it earlier: but there were still forty minutes.

The war? Goodness! It was thinking of his grandfather that had set his mind on those early days. Half a lifetime ago. For nearly all of the second half he had been a policeman. Interesting work the C.I.D. But twenty years had been long enough: he did not want to recall it. One way and another he had managed to save quite a lot of money: there had been ways of doing that: and now he was his own master. The antique shop suited him perfectly. It was there that he had met Lucy. She had come in to enquire the price of a rather embarrassed-looking Swansea cow. Urged by a sudden and most unusual impulse Morris had let her have it at a reduced price. Lucy had called again. Then he had been asked to lunch at Fitzroy Square to meet Lucy's husband, Matthew. And soon after that Matthew Werner had put him up for the Chesterfield Club. That had been a year ago. It seemed yesterday.

His election to the Chesterfield had given Morris acute pleasure. Moreover, after only six months, he had managed to get one of the permanently let bedrooms. The club was his home now and that, he thought, lent him a particular position. He did not want to recall the last twenty years of his life—though they had all gone to make him what he was, he supposed. The great thing was that he was a knowledgeable man in his new way of business. And he was a member of the Chesterfield. He could not have Lucy there, of course. But that was to the good. He didn't want the affair to get out of hand. He could be friendly with Matthew Werner at the club and friendly with Lucy somewhere else, when Matthew was away from town as he often was. As he was tonight. Tonight. Brent looked at his watch and asked for the bill.

While he waited Brent calculated in his head what it ought to be. He was not pleased to find that the folded paper, presently offered with a flourish on a saucer, was for £31.6. He had made it £216.6. He examined the bill narrowly. Couvert 2/6—ridiculous: that was the selective employment tax: all coming back on the consumer of Course. Coffee 2/-, that was up too—tax again. It was still 3/6 out—but no, he had forgotten the salad. So it was correct after all. Now there was the tip: 10%

of £31.6. was 6/2. Many people gave 12½% nowadays and that would be 7/8. Too much. Besides, as he often remarked, waiters don't respect you if you over-tip—they just think you're a fool. He couldn't leave 6/2. That, he conceded, would be mean. But he could leave 6/6. After a moment's further thought he decided on 7/-, and left the restaurant rather quickly.

A quarter past nine on an evening of early March, the snow of two days ago forgotten, spring in the air. He turned to the right up Dean Street, his mind so set on the immediate future that three ladies standing in doorways and two young men collecting customers for strip-tease shows did not even bother to address him. Walking quickly, but with eyes thoughtfully downcast, he crossed Oxford Street, and so set a course for Fitzroy Square by way of Rathbone Place and Charlotte Street.

Left to himself the ordinary person is not greatly observant. Thinking of something else, a man can pass a close friend in the street without seeing him. In general one sees what one expects to see. Detectives would not get very far if their victims recognized them as a matter of course. And yet, to anyone that knows, the plain clothes man is absurdly easy to identify. That neat suit: the careful tie: the awful little homburg hat with the small brim and the feather in the ribbon, the evident attempt to appear reasonably genteel. If you were expecting to see him you would spot him at once. But if you were not expecting to see him you might not see him at all. That is the point. Morris Brent knew all about plain clothes officers, whether of the police or of the agencies: but he took no notice at all of a man walking in the same direction as himself, a little behind him and on the other side of the street; a nondescript sort of a chap, neatly dressed, with a small-brimmed homburg hat with a feather in the ribbon. He looked as if he were on his way home to North Finchley. But he also had business in Fitzroy Square, and, long after Lucy Werner had opened her front door to Morris Brent, he still hung about the square, looking as though he were expecting a friend to keep an appointment. Indeed he stayed there for an hour until the same front door opened again and the same lady and Morris Brent came out together. Brent locked the door. The lady crossed the road to a small red Aston-Martin parked on the garden side of the square. Morris joined her. They had no luggage with them. But there was a small dressing-case on the back seat. The man in the awful little homburg had happened to notice that as he strolled up and down.

With the lady at the wheel the Aston-Martin moved off towards Regent's Park, and, as though such a firm action were a piece of advice to himself, the man standing in the square seemed to decide that it was not much use waiting any longer for his friend. He glanced at his watch and walked off to Warren Street underground station, where he got a ticket for home, which was not in North Finchley but somewhere in Pimlico.

As soon as he got there he put through a long-distance call to Amsterdam.

2

I

Dr. Davie and Miss Eggar were having breakfast together in the Principal's dining room. Before the fire the four cats sat ranged in a line like sphinxes.

"You examine the papers," said Miss Eggar' "and pass on to me the more succulent pieces of news."

"H'm . . ." said Davie, surveying the front page of one of three journals. "A child of six has written to the Queen. Someone called Miggins has run away from prison—which, given the opportunity, was very sensible of him. And the Prime Minister has declared that he has confidence in the good sense of the British people."

"I'm so glad about that," said Miss Eggar. "He was speaking frankly, I take it, and without fear or favour."

"Certainly he was."

"Anything else?"

"An American film star has married a fourth wife. There's a picture of him outside the registry office. I can never forgive a man who deliberately allows himself to be photographed kissing his wife. Can you? The assumption that others will enjoy witnessing the exercise is infinitely disgusting."

"I agree. Besides—the distortion of the nose is not something which ought to be recorded for future reference.

Dr. Davie helped himself to quince jelly. "How to describe this glorious colour?" he said, holding the jar up to the light. "It is red—but not the deep red of raspberry, nor the mushy red of strawberry, nor the bright red of currant It is red mellowed with gold—it's like a sunset."

"Well done," said Miss Eggar, neatly decapitating a boiled egg. "But how to describe its taste? It's Jacobean—Bacon ought to have written an essay about it."

Davie nodded his agreement. "Perhaps he did: it would have been called 'Of Quinces'." He returned to the paper. "Now here's a chap who has deliberately posed for his picture sucking a pipe. I dislike that as much as wife-kissing. It's so conceited. No properly brought up person enters another man's house smoking a pipe. Why should he suppose he gets away with it when he enters through the letter-box? He doesn't. One makes a note that the fellow is arrogant, self-satisfied and insensitive."

"Have some more coffee," said Miss Eggar.

"No thank you."

"I don't think you ought to read the papers, Dr. Davie. They must be a perpetual source of irritation."

"They are."

"Then put them down. It's time I took you across to the studio. Miss Cragg will be waiting to show you the works."

"And I want to see them," said Davie.

II

"This is astonishing," said Davie twenty minutes later. He had been watching George Tallent, the sound engineer, editing a poetry reading on tape.

"Not so astonishing as it looks," said George Tallent. "At the speed the tape runs a single syllable covers a sizable length of tape. One knows exactly where to cut."

"But your dexterity in putting it together again. It's very remarkable."

"Of course it is," said Miss Eggar. "Mr. Tallent likes to pretend it's quite simple, as all the best magicians do."

"Sometimes," said Miss Cragg, "he does make a mistake and snips off the beginning of a letter and then we enjoy the spectacle of George searching among the scraps on the floor for half a 'g' or the end of a 'p'. Usually he finds it and just sticks it back."

"I presume the idea of the editing is to create the best possible performance."

"Actors never give the same performance each time," said George Tallent. "If we record something three times each take is bound to contain something worth saving. We just make up a reading composed from all three. Sometimes we record a thing a dozen times—just picking out a word perhaps from one take, because it had some sort of colour lacking in the others."

"And the result," said Davie, "is something the artist didn't do, and possibly couldn't do—a performance the artist never quite gave."

"Well—yes."

24

"Dishonest—but I see the point."

"I don't see why 'dishonest'," said Miss Eggar. "It's an art in itself."

"It could lead to some interesting abuses," said Davie. "A tape wouldn't be very good evidence in a court of law if you can fiddle it as much as you say."

"There are limits," said Tallent. "You'd soon hear something wrong if you tried to insert something recorded in a different acoustic—or if you inserted an imitation of a voice. You can cut out a few words and insert the same voice saying something else. But you wouldn't get away with inserting a 'not' and reversing the sense. You'd do something to the rhythm."

"It's immensely interesting," said Davie. "Thank you for showing me."

"If you were to come back on March 10," said Miss Cragg, "we could show you the language course being recorded."

"Thank you—but I doubt if I could manage that."

"Of course you can't, Dr. Davie," said Miss Eggar.

"May I send you a copy of our last tape?" asked Miss Cragg.

"Yes, indeed—please do."

"I haven't got one here—and I'm afraid I've got to dash off now to lecture—but I'll send you one."

"To St. Nicholas's College, Cambridge, please. Goodbye. Many thanks."

"Goodbye—and thank you for the lecture."

"I have to be going too," said George Tallent. "Goodbye, sir. I've got to record Lady Minster opening a bazaar."

"And according to you it won't be any good my giving you my famous impersonation of that lady opening a bazaar."

"Afraid not, Dr. Davie."

"Pity," said Davie. "It has been much admired. Goodbye, Mr. Tallent—and thank you."

Miss Eggar was opening cupboards. "I don't know why Miss Cragg couldn't give you a tape," she said. "I suppose they've all gone and she's only got a file copy. But there's usually one hanging about." Miss Eggar pulled open a small drawer and peered into its innermost recess. "Aha!" she said. "What's this? Yes—here you are. This is the last issue. Do take it, Dr. Davie. Perhaps you wouldn't mind sending it back. It seems to be an only copy."

"Thank you," said Davie. "And that reminds me of something else. I hesitate to ask you—"

"You don't," said Miss Eggar. "You don't hesitate at all. And I know what you're going to say: you want to borrow—"

"Yes, please, I do. I got halfway through it last night and I simply must finish it."

"Halfway? That was quick going."

"I read quickly."

"But the Margaret Dunstable book, to which you doubtless refer—"

"Alas, no," said Davie. "I refer to Annabel Champion, as you very well know."

"You surprise me," said Miss Eggar. "Do take it—but kindly return it. I propose to read it myself the day after tomorrow."

Half an hour later Davie was speeding towards London, comfortably settled in a corner seat and deeply concerned with the brazen intuitions of Miss Murchiston. He had not the slightest idea that he had just put his great foot into an imbroglio not far removed from one of Miss Champion's prize entanglements.

III

There are two sorts of London clubs—those that inhabit what, in the days of the great and rich, were intended as elegant mansions; and those which inhabit great mausoleums deliberately erected for the purpose of sheltering a club. The hallmark of the mausoleum kind of club is to be found, very suitably, in the hall, which is by tradition decorated with the heads of stags and bison slain in the long past by sporting members who had gone to Africa to forget, or, in the absence of such trophies, by gloomy representations of animals and birds slaughtered nearer home and recorded in paintings of more than usually still life. Like sacrificial objects in the burial chambers of kings, the bison and the pictures seem to cater for the refreshment of members.

The Chesterfield was the other sort of club, housed in a still beautiful house erected for his delight in 1760 by Lord Bullivant and indeed long inhabited by his descendants until they took the knock in the 1920s.

It was half past eleven when Davie arrived in Vanburgh Street, Mayfair. Old Craddock, the hall porter, told him his room number and he was pleased to hear he had got what he had asked for—the room at the back on the first floor next to the library. The near-collegiate atmosphere of a gentleman's club (and a real gentleman's club: not a woman in sight except Miss Mittens, who reigned in splendour at the cash desk in the dining room) was very dear to Davie, and it was with a sense of anticipated satisfaction that he set off to his room. He loved the staircase at the Chesterfield with its elegant wrought iron banisters, the small Apollo at the half-landing, and the graceful Hermes presiding at the top of the stairs. Looking back to the hall he viewed with astonishment the polished dome of old Craddock shining in the sun. Then he moved right, opened a glass door and walked down a red-carpeted corridor. On the white walls was a line of Chinese paintings on rice paper. Davie was very attached to a stout and superbly feathered duck who was regarding his drab consort with a certain unmistakable look. In the eye of the lady was an equally unmistakable apprehension of impending duty. The situation, thought Davie, was exactly the same as that on Keats's Grecian Urn. "Thou still unravish'd bride of quietness."

However many members might have used the room since he was last at the club it seemed immediately to be his own. With an old pleasure he looked at the vermilion pictures on the toile de Jouy wallpaper, peeped out of the window, unpacked his case, laid *Who's For Murder?* on the chest of drawers, observed himself in the glass with regret, brushed his hair, and then stepped out again into the corridor. As he did so the library door opened. Willy Marchant stood framed against the morning.

"Ah! Davie! We don't see you very often."

"No, Marchant: I'm usually stuck in Cambridge. I'm just here for a night's self-indulgence at Covent Garden. Last night, by the way, my conversation was all of you. And this morning too."

"Eh? Me? How's that? Eh?"

Dr. Marchant pricked up his ears.

"Oh, yes. I was lecturing at St. Martha's College—the place that makes your English course. They were telling me all about it. Indeed I've been lent one of the tapes to listen to."

Willy Marchant's foxy face took on a look of embarrassment. His course was intended for foreigners, not for connoisseurs of the English language. He scented criticism, which was something he particularly disliked. In Willy Marchant's bosom was harboured a classic example of the inferiority complex, which does not mean (as most people believe) that a person thinks himself inferior, but that he fears that other people think him inferior. He disagrees. Willy Marchant disagreed: but the horrid speculation lingered.

"Have you? Have you indeed? I hope you will give it a good mark. It has been generally approved, I believe. Have you a tape machine?"

"I have at Cambridge."

"Ah—good, good. I haven't myself. You must tell me what you think of it. Goodbye. I have to go out and buy something—if only I can remember what it is. See you later no doubt."

Dr. Marchant knew very well what he wanted to buy—it was a toothbrush—but he was hoping to gain a reputation as an entertaining eccentric.

"Farewell," said Willy Marchant, and waving an elegant small hand he glided off along the corridor, giving a performance all the way to the glass door in the presumption that Davie was still looking at him. But Davie had gone into the library. It was empty. It usually was. He strolled over to the window. Below him lay an unexpected garden. In the center was a small gazebo. By its side a catalpa tree stretched one arm possessively above the roof. In the two far corners two fauns looked mischievously at each other. A little "camp"? thought Davie, remembering Miss Eggar's curtains.

The garden was reached by the french windows at the end of the dining room. In the summer the members of the Chesterfield would take their coffee there, sitting in the four loggias of the gazebo, or on a long garden seat at the end of the miniature lawn. But except for a gardener planting bulbs in November and sweeping up leaves in December it probably had not been entered by anyone for four or five months. In a week or two members might be using it again. Already the small lawn was squared by daffodils. For Davie the garden was a favourite secret place, for, except between two and three o'clock, or in high summer between eight and nine, it was entirely deserted. The mews, which in Lord Bullivant's time had sealed the end of the garden, had long been converted into expensive bijou residences. But their windows all looked the other way. The garden wall looked blankly at the club and saw nothing. Davie wished it was not still March. It was too cold for the garden. He made his way down the back stairs to the morning room.

It has been put about that the Chesterfield Club is famous for "brilliant conversation": which is unfortunate. It is an admirable club, but new or nervous members are intimidated by this agitating claim and continually apprehensive that their own contributions will be insufficiently dazzling. Some, indeed, are stricken permanently dumb for fear of falling below the expected standards, while the more extrovert members, confident

28

that the club's reputation must be founded on something, are easily convinced that it has in fact been derived from their own performances. There are thus at the Chesterfield Club a few royal talkers who command a sycophantic circle of listeners; and a good many other members who slink away into quiet rooms in order to escape from all the scintillation. Dr. Davie was one of the latter. It did not at all amuse him to be one of an audience, and he was not remotely inclined to command one.

Conway Gordon, principal raconteur of the Chesterfield, was already in full flow in the morning room.

"The trouble with the present day," he was saying as Davie came in, "is that no one has too little to do. The consequence is that letter-writing is a lost art. Hullo, Davie—don't you agree?"

"To what?" said Davie.

"To the proposition that letter-writing is a lost art."

Davie considered, then "No," he said, "I don't think I do. I don't believe anything is really lost. It may be mislaid, but someone turns it up sooner or later. One's told that no one can thatch any more; or make Honiton lace. But there always is one old man who does thatch, and he has a learning boy; and there always are earnest ladies who devote their lives to the rescue of pillow lace, or the rediscovery of parsnip wine. Surely anyone who set his mind to it could revive letter-writing. I must see. I've got some letters to write now. I'll tell you how I get on."

"Inspiration go with you," said Conway Gordon as Davie opened the door, on the other side of the room, leading to the hall. He added when Davie was out of hearing, "You can never catch that old devil out. He's always got an answer. He's wrong, of course; there are a lot of things that are lost—like the secret of mediaeval blue glass. There was a man who had a laboratory in a house on Clapham Common who thought he'd discovered the answer . . ."

In the hall a man in country tweeds was standing by the porter's cubbyhole asking old Craddock if there were any letters.

"Robbin!" said Davie. "My dear fellow, I'm delighted to see you. Where have you been? I've not seen you for at least eighteen months. You just disappeared."

Walter Robbin looked forty and was nearer fifty. Years ago he had been one of Davie's classical pupils. His eyes were blue as speedwells. His face was bronzed. He looked as if he were just up from the far west.

"Yes," he said. "I did precisely that. I'll tell you about it some time. I had to draw in my ears and economize."

"Economize? What a fearful thing! No operas? No Salzburg?"

"None of it. I've been in the country."

The glass pane in the front door sent a sudden flash of light across the hall. The man who came in had obviously been travelling. He handed a bag over the counter. "Take care of this, will you please, Craddock," he said. Then he added after a moment's silence, "Is Mr. Brent in?"

"I've not seen him, Sir Matthew."

Except that he was "Sir Matthew" Davie did not know who this member was. He said to Robbin, "Will you be in to lunch?"

"Yes."

"Let's sit together."

"Right"

"I must get some letters done."

"If he's not gone out he must be in," Sir Matthew was saying. "He lives here."

"Ah—but I mightn't have seen him, sir," said the aged Craddock. "What with the telephone . . ."

Davie closed the writing room door and heard no more of that. He sat down to compose a letter of politeness to Miss Eggar.

Presently the door opened. Out of the corner of his eye he could see that Sir Matthew had entered the room. He took a newspaper and sat down. Two minutes later he got up and exchanged it for a magazine. Two minutes later he got up and stood beside one of the long windows that looked into the street. He was a good-looking man of perhaps forty. Davie considered he was a great fidget.

The writing table at which Davie was sitting stood opposite a second long window looking into the street. He had just finished addressing his letter to Miss Eggar when he heard the man at the other window utter a soft exclamation. Davie glanced at him, and seeing that he was staring at something outside, down the street to the right, he looked in the same direction. A small red car was drawn up at the curb, about a dozen yards short of the club door. A man got out and there was a minute while he stooped down to smile and say goodbye to the driver. Then the red car drove off down the street. As it passed the club windows Davie noticed that a lady with golden hair was sitting at the wheel. He also noticed that the man who was approaching the club was someone he knew slightly: Brent, Morris Brent: Davie had occasionally sat next to him at lunch at the long table and had found him agreeable. Then he remembered that Brent had once been very loquacious about a new tape recorder. He felt

Miss Eggar's tape in his pocket. Why shouldn't he ask him? He went into the hall as Brent opened the front door.

Brent, who was looking uncommonly elated, said good morning in a breezy way, as it were to the club in general.

"Good morning," said Davie. "Brent—forgive my bothering you, but I wonder if you'd do me a favour. I believe you have a tape recorder thing."

"Yes."

"I want to play a short tape. Could you oblige me? It would be most kind."

"Certainly, Davie." Normally Morris Brent called everybody by their Christian names on the first time of meeting—but he had never discovered Davie's first name. Few people had. He was Dr. R. V. Davie in the club list, and anyhow there was something about Davie which postponed that sort of familiarity. So "Certainly, Davie," said Morris Brent. "I'll be delighted." And this was true. Any contact that might be useful was a pleasure to Morris Brent.

"That's very good of you."

"Not a bit. Delighted. When? Now?"

"Is it convenient?"

"Perfectly," said Brent. "Come along."

They turned towards the stairs. As they did so the writing room door opened. Davie moved slowly on up the stairs, but "Matthew!" said Brent, suddenly halted. "I thought you were abroad."

"So did I," said the man in the doorway. "I came back."

For a second Brent seemed stuck for a word, then, with one foot on the stairs he said, "Let's have a talk later. I'm terribly busy at the moment Will you be here for lunch?"

"No, I shan't."

If Brent had been taken by surprise he had recovered remarkably quickly. It was the other way about with his friend. He seemed to have stepped into the hall resolved on a particular course and then to have checked as though he did not know how to proceed.

"I'll be here all the afternoon," said Morris Brent, mounting the stairs.

At the half-landing Davie looked back into the hall. The man called Matthew was staring upwards watching the retreating figure of Morris Brent. But it was not only Matthew's face that caught Davie's attention. Robbin had come into the hall, and stood, looking upwards, as though suddenly surprised. Behind him, standing by the morning room door, was Conway Gordon. Perhaps following Robbin, he too glanced

31

upwards. And so for three seconds three members of the Chesterfield Club stood like a tableau at the curtain-fall of the second act of an old melodrama. And then the front door burst open and in came Sam Coppin with a guest. The hall became loud with jocularities. They could still hear Coppin's laughter as they turned right at the head of the stairs, opened the glass door and walked along the red-carpeted corridor, past Davie's room and past the library, to a door at the end on the left.

"Who was that chap you spoke to in the hall?" asked Davie.

"Werner—Matthew Werner. An old friend of mine. Here we are. Come in."

Brent's room, facing into the street, was large and square and had once been the conjugal bedchamber of the first Lord Bullivant. In the right hand corner a door led into what had once been Lady Bullivant's powder closet. At the end of the 19th century in the glorious days when Violet, fourth Lady Bullivant, was commonly supposed (and rightly) to be the mistress of a royal personage, it was turned into a bathroom. Since the Chesterfield bought the house, thirty-five years ago, the room had suffered a further alteration and a degradation. It now had a door of its own into the passage, which meant that it was not, and was not intended to be, for the wholly private use of the occupier of the room. When an outsider used it he bolted the bedroom door on the bathroom side. He could, and usually did, forget to unbolt it when he went out: unclubbable behaviour which greatly affronted Morris Brent, who liked to regard the bathroom as his personal property.

Brent set up the tape. "You must excuse me if I shave," he said. "I was up early."

"Carry on," said Davie.

It was the usual kind of language course. Willy Marchant had conceived nothing new. Two young people were supposed to be visiting London. Evidently in previous editions they had arrived, gone to a hotel, been to a restaurant, gone out shopping. In this one they were at the theater, and the lesson was concentrated a good deal on the conditional.

"I would like to put my coat in the cloakroom." "Would you like a programme?" And so on.

The tape drew to a conclusion on a note of gallantry. "I would like to go to the theater with you again," said the young man. "When could you come?" And without pausing for a moment's bashful consideration the young woman replied, "I shall be free on Wednesday, the fourth." "I shall look forward to that," said the young man, and then the tape faded out on the last bars of "La donna è mobile."

Brent stopped the tape, wound it back a little way, and played the last bit again. "That's comic," he said, and, winding the tape back again, he played it a third time.

"Delightfully inappropriate," said Davie.

"It reminds me," said Brent, "of the old phrase-book joke about 'Our postillion has been struck by lightning'."

"I've never been able to decide," said Davie, "was that put in with total dullness of wit, or was the compiler in fact making a little joke? Are we the fools? I remember once rocking with laughter at some Victorian photographs, and my mother painfully explaining that they were *meant* to be funny. Apparently in the first freshness of photography it was considered a lark to make up absurdly posed groups. We're inclined to miss the jokes of our parents. 'Our postillion has been struck by lightning' was a sound example of a grammatical construction. The phrase-book would only have been duller, not better if it had read 'Our postillion has been sent to Geneva.' Here we have an ardent little scene dissolving into 'La donna è mobile'—which is funny, but perhaps Willy Marchant meant it to be funny."

"No," said Brent, "Willy Marchant never meant anything to be that."

Davie laughed. "Poor Willy," he said. "He means well."

"But surely that's the worst—"

"Don't say it," said Davie. "Most people mean rather less than well. A much worse thing to say about anyone is that he does something or other 'in his own right.' That means he hasn't made the grade. One doesn't say for instance that Milton was a poet in his own right."

"That's a point," said Brent. "O.K. Let's say Willy Marchant is an educationalist in his own right."

"Mr. Brent," said Davie, getting up, "you are uncharitable and rather naughty—but thank you very much for your kindness."

Brent, who had been rewinding the tape, handed it to Davie. "Not a bit," he said, crossing the room to the bathroom. The door was bolted. "Blast!" he growled. "They're always doing that. Bolt the door and leave it bolted. It never strikes them—"

"There's someone in there," said Davie. "Or there was. I heard someone go in just after you started the tape."

"Did you? I didn't. What on earth for? It's nearly lunch time."

"He doesn't seem to be having a bath," said Davie. "Perhaps he's gone again."

"That's what I mean. It's so—"

"Ah, Brent—man is vile: we know that. I must be going. I'm greatly obliged to you. Thank you very much."

"Staying long?"

"No, only the night. I'm going to Covent Garden."

"So am I," said Brent. "Perhaps we'll see each other."

Davie let himself out into the corridor. The bathroom door, he noticed, was open. He stepped back, and drew the offending bolt. Then he continued on his way towards the stairs.

As he reached the glass door at the end of the corridor another glass door on the opposite side of the landing opened just sufficiently to permit the passage of a tall thin man, who peered out with an absurd sort of caution before stepping out on the landing. It was Frederick Dyke, famous for his habit of entering and leaving rooms through the smallest possible aperture as though he were a spy in a film. Indeed there were those who did not hesitate to hint that he *was* a spy. He was known to be able to talk Russian. He had once had great interests in the East. Perhaps he still had. He was said to be immensely rich, and to possess a fabulous collection of pictures which he kept very much to himself in a house in Putney. Indeed, when any sufficiently valuable picture was stolen from one of the national collections, the more facetious members of the Chesterfield always assumed that Frederick Dyke had it under lock and key in his attics. He was not greatly inclined to bestow his friendship. Davie had held an uneasy acquaintance with him for some years, not because he was a member of the Chesterfield, but because he was a tireless collector of operas. That meant that he was to be seen not just at Covent Garden, Sadlers Wells and Glyndebourne, but also at obscure productions in Town Halls, put on for two performances on stages with no flies, no depth and no wings: and yet put on. Thus had Dyke and Davie both seen early works of Handel, Verdi, Puccini, Rossini, and, from time to time, even discussed them in intervals over pale cups of coffee in huge and hideous rooms, mysteriously designed by Edwardian architects with the same lack of apparent purpose as they had lavished on the equipment of their stages. So Davie said, "Hullo, Dyke." And Dyke, approaching, said, "Staying here?" And Davie said, "Yes, I've got the room next to the library—my favourite."

"Ah, I see."

Dyke spoke as though he thought Davie's information was of peculiar, almost public interest.

"For a moment I wondered where you had sprung from," he said. "But I see—you're staying here. I do a certain amount of work in the library. It is quiet. The club hasn't a great many rival scholars. Except of course Willy Marchant."

His face relaxed in a lean smile. Somehow nobody ever spoke of Willy Marchant without suggesting that he was in some way ridiculous.

"He works at his language course in there and sometimes I am privileged to be shown the results."

It was on the tip of Davie's tongue to say that he too had been so privileged: but they had reached the head of the stairs and the subject did not seem a particularly profitable one. So he said, "I take it I shall see you at *Edgar*."

"My goodness, yes," said Dyke. "Both performances. We shall never see it again."

"Good morning, gentlemen."

Captain Blonde, the club secretary, was coming down the stairs behind them.

Davie thought Blonde was the best dressed man he knew. He was good-looking, too, though the total effect was a little spoiled by the eyes, which were of that opaque blue more turquoise than sapphire. It is a cold unyielding colour. Blonde was an excellent secretary. He was not a "boon companion". But perhaps he reserved his companionship for the fair sex. He was said to be a great lady-keeper.

"Good morning, Blonde," said Davie, halting on the half-landing. But Dyke, just raising his hand in acknowledgement, went on down into the hall. He was not given to passing the time of day with anybody, and certainly not with Captain Blonde, who was affable but not learned in anything that engaged the mind of Frederick Dyke. Nobody expected anything else from Dyke; indeed his oddities were in general rather cherished as an added attraction to the amenities of the Chesterfield.

It was one o'clock. There were a number of members in the hall. As he moved towards the dining room Davie noticed Willy Marchant coming down the stairs, giving his performance of the preoccupied scholar reluctantly dragged from his studies for the refreshment of the tyrant stomach.

"Exhausted Nature for refreshment calls," Davie murmured, silently completing in his head the ribald couplet he had first heard as an undergraduate.

Evidently Willy had remembered what he wanted to buy and had made his way back to the library to continue with the English Course, Part Eight.

"Boon companion," thought Davie as he moved down the corridor. What an absurd word! A Gallicism no doubt. He made a mental note to look it up.

Robbin was waiting for Davie at the long table in the dining room.

"Tell me your news," said Davie.

"No—tell me yours. I've been in the country. What's been happening in the opera world?"

"The air has hummed with all the usual rumours and scandals. And in the winter there was one very entertaining affair. The man Malcolm Williamson wrote an opera that was full of tunes. This, as you may suppose, flung the musical world into a tizzy. Some of the critics, unable to deny that they had enjoyed themselves, felt none the less that a rebuke was necessary: while several fellow composers plainly considered that Williamson had acted in a very underhand manner. The general public were of course entranced, both by the controversy and by the opera. You must go. It's bound to be revived."

"I read something about it in my sylvan retreat," said Robbin.

"Which was?"

"Exmoor. I've been living in a small pub. Fishing while it was on. Walking when it wasn't. And writing."

"Publishable? Or libellous?"

"Libellous, I think. I've been getting some venom out of my glands. It's done me good."

Davie said no more on that. Robbin seemed physically well: but he looked worried.

George Canteloupe lowered his enormous bulk on to the chair next to Davie.

"Hullo—glad to see you here again. I thought you usually bestowed yourself on the Gainsborough."

"I do when I've got things to do at the museum. The bedroom I like there is being done up. If they cover it with stars and rectangles I shall leave."

"Good," said Canteloupe. "How's Cambridge? I always think of you shovelling down crème brûlée."

"It is a solemn fact that the only place you will get a proper crème brûlée is in a Cambridge college—or, I must frankly allow, in an Oxford one. You see it sometimes on a London menu—but if they do know how to make it they certainly don't try."

"What do they do wrong?"

"They dishonourably make the custard with milk and then vilely bake it in the oven."

"The swine!" said George Canteloupe. "Do they really? Tell me how it ought to be made, Davie, and I'll see if I can browbeat my cook into doing it."

"I'm not sure, Canteloupe, that I ought to introduce a man of your figure to the pleasures of crème brûlée—I feel a certain responsibility."

"Hell to that," said George Canteloupe. "If you don't give me the recipe I shall disclose to Conway Gordon the story about you and the widow at Monte Carlo."

"You reveal yourself in a very unpleasant light, Canteloupe. You shall have the recipe."°

Davie was sitting at one end of the long table, Canteloupe on his left, Robbin on his right. At the opposite end Conway Gordon presided. The table was full except for one place, next but one to Gordon—on Robbin's side of the table. Then Morris Brent came in. Glancing at Davie as he passed, he moved on down the room to the vacant seat.

Robbin turned to Davie. "Who was that chap?" he asked.

"Brent—Morris Brent."

"I don't remember seeing him here before."

"You've been away. He's a fairly new member—an antique expert, I believe. Do you know, Canteloupe?"

"He's in the antique world," said Canteloupe. "Whether he's an expert I wouldn't care to say. I believe he used to be a policeman—detective of some kind."

"Oh?" said Davie.

"Yes," said Canteloupe. "Why not? For my part I'd as soon hobnob with a retired policeman as with an active city gent. The former at least—"

"We see your point," said Davie.

"You don't," said Canteloupe, "—not all of it. But I won't elaborate here." Then, without consulting the menu, he ordered the treacle tart. Members of the Chesterfield Club were never likely to be confronted by a bastard crème brûlée, but the chef did make a dream of a treacle tart.

"For me too, please," said Davie.

° Dr. Davie's recipe for crème brûlée can be found at the end of this volume.

The club had been unusually full that day, but twenty minutes later the room was nearly empty and the last few members were filing past the little box where Miss Mittens held her court. The Chesterfield gentlemen always behaved with great gallantry towards Miss Mittens, and Miss Mittens always behaved with great dignity towards them. She accepted their cash as a queen might have accepted the tributes of her liege subjects, and when she had collected it all she popped it into a tin cash box, let herself out of her cage, inclined her head gracefully towards Wilkin, the head waiter, and lost no time in conveying her riches to the security of the secretary's office upstairs—a journey always tinged with excitement for Miss Mittens, who had seen more westerns about the raiding of banks and trains and saloons than most people, and never tired of her daily adventure up the empty stairway of the Chesterfield Club at about half past two in the afternoon.

The secretary's office and the secretary's room occupied, on the other side of the house, a complementary position to the library and Davie's bedroom. So at the top of the staircase, by the statue of Hermes, Miss Mittens turned left, opened the second glass door and entered upon a second red-carpeted corridor. Here the white walls exhibited cartoons by Spy, pictures more familiar on the walls of clubs than the Chinese paintings on rice paper which gave Davie so much satisfaction. She particularly liked the one of Sir Charles Villiers Stanford, because of "Stanford in B♭", which she had heard so often at St. Michael's in the days of the old choirmaster. Nowadays, of course, it was Vaughan Williams, which, frankly, she did not like as well.

Miss Mittens opened the office door. Seated behind his large table, Mr. Ambrose, the steward and cashier, was awaiting her. Miss Mittens handed over her charge.

"There we are, Mr. Ambrose," she said.

"Thank you, Miss Mittens."

"It was a more than usually crowded dining room today," said Miss Mittens, "which makes me a little late."

Then, like the Lady of Shalott, she crossed the room to the window and looked down on the daffodils.

"Oh!" said Miss Mittens. "Spring has really come. One of the members has ventured into the garden."

"He'll regret it," said Mr. Ambrose. "It's not warm enough." But Miss

Mittens regarded the garden with an indulgent smile as she swiftly built a little story in her mind in which she descended the fire escape outside the window, and crossed the lawn as though by accident to the gazebo. How surprised he would be!

"Is a certain person in?" said Miss Mittens, returning to Mr. Ambrose's table and pointing a genteel finger towards the secretary's room next door to the office.

"No," said Mr. Ambrose.

"Well—I'll be getting on," said Miss Mittens. "I don't want to be caught. I'm late as it is."

V

There had been no one about when Robbin re-entered the dining room at twenty-five minutes to three. Sounds of washing-up proceeded from the kitchen premises beyond the screened doorway, but the dining room was empty, already tidy and set for dinner.

He crossed the room to the french windows, opened them carefully and quietly, stepped into the garden, and drew the windows to behind him. The day had become unexpectedly warm. It was surprising that no one else had decided to inspect the garden: but no one had.

From the window to his right came the click of billiard balls, and that strange cry familiar to indoor sportsmen, the hoot of incredulity which greets a shot the player pretends to be calculated and the onlookers decide to be accidental. There was a mesh across the lower half of the billiards room window. It was improbable, he thought, that anyone there had seen him enter the garden. The eyes of the people in a billiards room are usually engaged in following the game. He glanced up at the higher windows. No one was looking out.

He sat down in the gazebo in the section facing the sun and the blind looking backs of the houses in the next street. He had come there because there was a problem on his mind, and because—until he resolved it—he did not want to be engaged suddenly in a difficult conversation. He was not well pleased, therefore, when, about five minutes later, he heard the sound of somebody else opening the french windows, followed by foot-steps on the gravel path. If there had been time he would have moved quietly into the small loggia on the narrow side of the gazebo. But clearly there was not time, so he crossed his legs, folded his arms and waited.

The fact that he now heard nothing did not mean that the person had halted. It meant that he had stepped on to the grass.

But Miss Mittens understood nothing of this. She had seen only one of the garden's visitors. A moment later Miss Mittens was on her way down the red-carpeted corridor. She had a date with a friend at the Academy Cinema.

VI

Matthew Werner had gone out to lunch because he was resolved to quarrel with Morris Brent. By suggesting a meeting at lunch time Brent had obviously hoped to postpone an argument. Matrimonial problems are not to be discussed in a club dining room. Werner was not going to be diverted by that maneuver, and so, after spending twenty minutes with his barber in Dover Street, there he was at Berto's, Shepherd Market, only a short walk from the Chesterfield, eating a solitary meal, and not enjoying it, nervously wasting time until he could return in the quiet part of the afternoon and find Brent alone.

While he was drinking his coffee he wrote a four-line letter to his wife, and with the aid of a large tip persuaded Berto to have it sent immediately to Fitzroy Square. By that time it was two-thirty. He decided to stay until two-forty. But even when he had left Berto's he deliberately lingered, to peer first at a print shop and then at a window full of undistinguished junk. He had told himself that he would confront Brent at about three o'clock. But the fact was that he was on edge. Brent had a gift for talking. He was sure to get the best of an argument. He was also an adept liar. Matthew Werner advanced but slowly on the Chesterfield Club. He was determined to have a showdown—but was this the best time to have it, after all? The fact that he recognized his own hesitations, and knew them for weakness, did not make it any easier.

Not long after he was back at Berto's.

The last customers had gone, and the small low room had put on that dead look that an empty restaurant always wears. The smart green table-cloths were awry. Crumpled napkins lay on the chairs. There were crumbs on the floor. Even the baskets of fruit had somehow assumed the aspect of theatrical properties.

"Ullo, Sir Matthew," said Berto, emerging from behind a curtain in his shirt sleeves. "Lost somethink?"

"Yes, Berto," said Werner. "I had a book. It was under the chair."

"A book? This chair, wasn't it? There is nothink there, Sir Matthew. Guiseppe, was there a book?"

"I didn't see none, sir," said Guiseppe.

"Really! The honesty of your customers, Berto—"

"Are you sure you had it, Sir Matthew?"

"I had it all right. But don't bother. I shall never know now 'who did it'—but it's not worth making a fuss about."

"I am so sorry, Sir Matthew."

"It doesn't matter."

Matthew Werner looked at his watch, and this time he pulled himself together. He had been glad of the excuse to return to Berto's, but now he suddenly felt differently about everything. He was no longer anxious. He went straight back to the Chesterfield.

"Is Mr. Brent in?" he asked Craddock.

"I haven't seen him go out, Sir Matthew."

"Good. I'll find him."

It was three-thirty. First we went to the billiards room. It was empty. Then he went upstairs and knocked on Brent's door. There was no reply. Then he looked in at the library and received an unfriendly stare from Frederick Dyke. Then he looked in at the card room and the writing room. As he crossed the hall again he said to Craddock, "I very much want to see Mr. Brent. If he comes in, please tell him I'm in the morning room."

VII

The science of Life (a Cambridge hedonist has proclaimed) depends on the placing of tea as near as possible to the ceremony of luncheon. Two o'clock to four is the dead time; the second part of the day does not begin until it is wakened by tea. Davie agreed with the hedonist, but he also considered it reasonable that he and the day should suffer from exhaustion in company. At least between a quarter to three and four o'clock he liked to lie down, and he made a particular point of doing so on a night when he was going to the opera. So, a little after Miss Mittens mounted the stairs, casting a routine look over her shoulder at the half-landing to see that she was not being followed, Davie had walked slowly up to the first floor. His first object was the library: he needed a book even if he were going to drop asleep over it. Frederick Dyke was sitting in the wing armchair in the window, supporting a large folio on his knees. He looked up at Davie over the top of his glasses and said never a word. Davie said nothing in reply. They both understood how to behave in a library.

Davie knew what he wanted and a minute later, a volume of Sir Thomas Browne in his hand, he closed the door quietly behind him. Then he took four steps up the corridor to his own room, undressed, and slipped luxuriously between the sheets. He firmly believed in making a complete exercise of lying down. Dropping off in a chair was quite pleasant but it was not enough. Lying on top of the bed or even under the eiderdown was draughty: you had to take your coat and shoes off and, if there wasn't something wrapped round the end of you, your feet got cold: besides you can't lie comfortably if you're wearing braces. No, the proper thing was to take it all off. The sheets were deliciously cool: the room was warm: Davie laid Sir Thomas Browne respectfully on the bedside table, and closed his eyes. He did not open them again till a quarter past four, which was later than he intended.

He regretted the days of evening dress de rigueur, but, since nowadays so small a proportion of men wore dinner jackets at Covent Garden, Davie went with the majority when he was only up for the night. But he took care always to wear a dazzling white shirt and a discreetly blue tie. Indeed he almost looked "dressed" and almost felt "dressed"—but what folly! he used to think: you had to change into something: what was the point in insisting on a blue suit rather than a black one?

It was nearly twenty-five to five when he opened his bedroom door. At the end of the corridor Frederick Dyke with accustomed caution was in the act of opening the glass door. He turned round as he heard Davie approaching behind him.

"There you are again," he said severely.

"Ah," said Davie, "you and I are like clocks. Time for lunch, time for tea, and we climb out of our bolt-holes."

"With the difference," said Dyke, "that I have been working and you have been sleeping."

"Too true: and now, as soon as I've had tea, a slave to pleasure, I'm going to Covent Garden."

"*Turandot*: I don't like the sets or the clothes."

"They do at least suggest the right period. I dislike this modern kink for presenting works precisely as they were not intended. *Rosenkavalier* in art nouveau scenery is twaddle."

"Has anyone ever done it the other way round?" said Dyke. "Let me see—a Tudor production of *The Importance of Being Earnest*—that would be 'original'."

"What a splendid thought!" said Davie, and added "I'm going to *Turandot* because I approve of Shuard."

"Why are you going so early?" said Dyke.

"I like to walk there. The ignoble strife of the madding crowd amuses me. And then I shall dine nearby."

Davie had booked a table at L'Opéra for six o'clock. He left the Chesterfield at a quarter past five, and ambled along Piccadilly, watching the neon signs competing with the twilight, glancing nostalgically across the road at the Ritz and with pleasure at the black and gold ironwork of Barclay's Bank, pausing in front of travel agencies and wondering if he wanted to go to Egypt or Australia and what he would make of a package tour of Ibizia for £37 10. and what precisely the 10/- might be for.

The first thing he noticed as he skirted the north side of the circus was that the wax lady was no longer in the Invisible Mending shop and indeed the Invisible Mending shop no longer occupied its familiar premises. The site was occupied by an emporium of souvenirs and greeting cards. Davie felt gravely shocked. She had been there only a few months before. He went in and asked the young lady who presided over the greeting cards what had happened. "They've given up," she said. "Not gone anywhere."

Davie looked round the little box, lined and impedimented with stacks of ready-phrased greetings, and marvelled at the baseness of human nature. Fifty years had the wax lady sat in the window, bending over her work with her gentle smile. He remembered in the late twenties when the short man, the tall man, and the fat man who had stood for years on the pediment of Horne Brothers in Shaftesbury Avenue, clad only in vest and pants, had been ruthlessly destroyed in the process of rebuilding. The vandals would stop at nothing. It was said that it had taken royal intervention to preserve the red lion of Waterloo, now white and transported to a site near Westminster Bridge. No royal voice had spoken for the three men in vests and pants and now one of the most endearing relics of early 20th century London had been spirited away without a word of protest from anyone. "What Cambyses and Time hath spared avarice now consumeth," murmured Davie. "Pardon?" said the young lady. "Nothing," said Davie. "Thank you for telling me."

But how impossible it is to write history, he was thinking as he threaded his way through the repulsive crowds of Coventry Street. How many people had noticed her going? How many had cared? Who would remember her in a year's time? And she had lent her gracious presence to the circus for more than fifty years. The fickleness, the indifference, the sightlessness of the public was frightening. No one would notice if they removed the Scot from Carlyle's Retreat, or the naval officer with the sextant from the shop in Brompton Road.

Feeling justly indignant, Davie crossed the Charing Cross Road and escaped into Long Acre, so quiet now, but still decorated by a few dilapidated oranges, and the odd helping of cabbage, witnesses of the day's excitements but fallen by the way like drunks after a party. In an empty shop window a guardian cat lay curled up asleep in the lamp-light. Behind it a greengrocer's notice proclaimed the desirability of "Juicy Spanish Navels". This cheered him up considerably, and presently he was renewing his pleasure at the stately delights of L'Opéra. He liked the green and gold chairs and the golden fringes on the red tablecloths, and the playbills on the walls and the spectacular posters of Bernhardt by Mucha. And there were several things he liked on the menu.

VIII

At the same hour in her bedroom on the second floor of the house in Fitzroy Square Lucy Werner was taking twice as long as usual (and that was long) to prepare herself for Covent Garden. She had had her bath. She only had to slide into a green satin dress, choose the right earrings and finish her makeup. But at six-fifteen she was still sitting at her dressing table in a pink gown and staring in the looking glass sometimes at herself, sometimes at a letter that lay just below it and was equally reflected there.

The letter was from her husband. It had arrived by hand in the early afternoon; but she had not found it until she came home at four o'clock.

Berto's Restaurant 2.15 p.m.

Dear Lucy—I came back from Holland early today. Apart from what I have been told, I happen to have seen you myself when you delivered Morris Brent at the Chesterfield this morning. I am expecting to see him this afternoon. In the meantime I shall not be returning to Fitzroy Square.

Matthew

Lucy Werner was very angry. She had never imagined that her affair with Morris could end in the smallest inconvenience to herself. If there had been a row surely the first thing he ought to have done was to ring her up and warn her. He had done nothing at all. He had just left her to find it out for herself. It was disgusting, cowardly. In the last two hours she had rung up the Chesterfield six times. Mr. Brent was not in. He was not in his room. He had not left any message. He had not telephoned. The last time she rang she had asked for her husband. Sir Matthew had been at the club, said old Craddock, since about three-thirty or there-abouts, but he had just gone out.

It was typical of Lucy Werner that in the midst of her vexation she was able to remember that she had her own opera ticket. Luckily the fool had given her that "in case anything happens." It had happened all right and she would have something blistering to say about it in the interval. And then it occurred to her that if Morris had had a row with Matthew perhaps he might not even come. And if that happened she wouldn't know where she stood until she could find him. If he'd ratted on her—gone away—told Matthew the truth . . . She looked again at the letter. "Apart from what I have been told"—what non-sense! Told what and by whom? And what did it matter her bringing Morris to the club? It was twelve o'clock: why shouldn't she give a friend a lift? Matthew was a jealous fool: he couldn't possibly have any evidence. Lucy Werner was not the kind of woman who twists the truth into any shape suitable to her purpose: she did not pretend that there was no evidence: she simply did not believe that Matthew knew how to find it.

A little gold clock, which pertly displayed its private parts under the protection of a glass dome, chimed quietly on the mantelpiece. It was half past six. She rang L'Opéra and asked if Mr. Brent had arrived. He had not.

Lucy decided to go direct to the opera house. She detested sand-wiches, she detested hanging about alone at Covent Garden (women of her looks never do that) but she was not going to be stood up by Morris Brent. She telephoned for a taxi, put on the green dress, screwed in her emerald earrings and finished her face. As she went downstairs the tele-phone began to ring. Lucy hesitated. Then she turned down the corners of her mouth. It was something she did too often. She had made herself little lines there which would grow up to be permanent symbols of discontent. But though Lucy wanted to ignore the telephone it was something she could never persuade herself to do. She went into the sitting room and picked up the receiver.

"Yes?" Lucy employed an ice-cold tone which she had been inwardly practising since five o'clock.

"Can I speak to Mr. Emery, please?" said a bright little voice in her ear.

"Mr. Emery!" said Lucy. "No—you can't. Certainly not."

She slammed the telephone down and let herself out of the front door. The taxi was waiting.

IX

Davie always sat in the stalls and he liked to get the same seat. He had found one on the left of the left-hand gangway, near the front, which gave him an entirely free view of the stage, and he was so used to sitting in it that he felt twisted if by some misfortune he found himself on the other side of the house. There were a lot of other people who had favourite seats, some of whom he had seen so often over the years that he felt he knew them intimately. "The count" was presumably dead: he had not been seen for at least three years. He used to wear frilly shirts and cuffs and white gloves and rings and an opera cloak; and he never spoke to anybody. Davie had been fond of the count. At the other end of the scale was a garrulous woman who made a point of coming to the opera in trousers. He liked to suppose that she wore a skirt at home.

Davie sat down, looked at his programme and then let his eyes rove over the house. It was full. There were people in the slips. There were people standing at the back of the stalls circle. In front of him was old Mrs. Hanter, and her attendant daughter. Behind him was that group of jolly young men who always applauded so loudly that Davie had sometimes wondered if they were professionally engaged for the purpose. Glancing up over his left shoulder Davie scanned the stalls circle. In the front row were two people whom he had seen for years and always in the same seats. Next to them was a handsome woman in a green dress. Davie thought she looked cross. There was an empty seat next to her, and the auditorium lights were dimming. Probably her husband was late and there would be a lot of "Really" and "But surely" and "I do think" in the interval. But now the audience was applauding and the conductor threaded his way through the pit, shook hands with the leader and bowed.

The splendid ritual had begun.

Davie never liked to miss any of the entertainments and experiences which Covent Garden affords. In the second interval he made his way up the little side stairs and then around the back of the Grand Circle to the crush bar, which is always a kind of thermometer reflecting not only the warmth of the audience, but the sort of audience. On some nights, a *Madame Butterfly* night perhaps, it will not be crowded, a large number of that opera's supporters seeming to be content to remain in their seats: and the conversation will not be brisk, perhaps because there is not much more to be said about *Madame Butterfly*. But on other nights—at a Strauss Opera, say, or a Zeffirelli production, the place will be jammed, and the air loud with excited talk. The talk is not necessarily about the opera, but the occasion produces the atmosphere.

Tonight the room was packed and, as he did not propose to contend for a drink, Davie stood on the stairs inside the room and surveyed the throng, ravenously intent upon the business of refreshment. It was a maneuver which saved him from an unwelcome encounter. Looking over the banisters he was suddenly vouchsafed a unique view of the dark parting in Dr. Marie Baendels's golden crown, and even in those open spaces he received the benison of the scented cloud that encircled her. And then Davie remembered where he had seen her before—at Sadlers Wells. She, too, was an opera-goer. He watched her tacking her way towards the closed end of the room where, in safe harbour, she came to anchor by a man who was evidently expecting her. He had a drink waiting for her.

Davie came down the stairs and made his way through the crowd in the opposite direction till he found himself successfully squeezed out at the head of the Grand Staircase.

As you descend those noble steps you see yourself flanked in flowers in the great looking glass. It was a revelation that always made Davie throw his shoulders back. It was shaming to be shown how easily one stooped and poked. He had just completed this discipline when, at the foot of the staircase, he ran into Lady Meade-Fuller, who was wearing, he noticed, a more than usually bizarre evening dress of sage green and purple.

"My dear R.V.!" said Lady Meade-Fuller, "*How* delightful to see you! This *is* a surprise." George Canteloupe once said that Mildred Meade-Fuller went in for good-gracious living. She was always so delightfully surprised to see everybody else. It was an amiable characteristic and Davie liked her.

"You shouldn't be surprised," he said. "This, my dear Mildred, is my natural habitat."

"Yes, yes, my dear, I know. And how is Cambridge?"

"Next term someone's going to put on an opera by a 19th-century composer no one's ever heard of."

"My dear, how very exciting!"

"Apparently it was found in an old trunk."

"How entirely delightful!" said Mildred Meade-Fuller. "It's bound to be a great success. I shall come of course."

"And of course you will have lunch with me," said Davie.

"My dear, how very kind! I shall be delighted."

Several men were standing about in the foyer with coats over their arms. "They aren't leaving," said Davie. "They think it's unseemly to enter the auditorium with their coats at the start of the performance: so they check them in—but they don't want to be caught in the crush at the end, so they check them out in the interval and *do* carry them into the auditorium. They like to be correct to begin with but sensible when it comes to the rub."

"Blissfully illogical," said Mildred Meade-Fuller: "but when you think of the appalling inadequacies of English cloakrooms—"

"Tell me who that is," said Davie. "She really *is* leaving."

"Where?"

"The green dress and the mink coat."

"That's Lady Werner."

"Bless me—only this morning I was asking who her husband was. He belongs to my club."

"They come here a lot."

"She's been here alone tonight—sitting by an empty seat."

"I hate that myself," said Mildred Meade-Fuller; "which reminds me I don't know what's happened to Francis. No, there he is. Goodbye, R.V. What a delightful surprise seeing you!"

"Goodbye, Mildred."

And this was the end of that encounter for the bell was ringing and the lights had been dimmed in the foyer. Everyone was surging back to their places, the gentlemen with overcoats over their arms far more conspicuous than if they had brought them in in the first place.

As Davie walked around the circular foyer and up the short stairs to the stalls he found himself thinking of Morris Brent and Matthew Werner in the hall at the Chesterfield. Brent had said he was coming to Covent Garden. Davie had not seen him. Was it Matthew Werner who had failed to turn up? Or was Brent the escort who should have been sitting with Lady Werner? And what did it matter anyway?

Davie always waited for the curtain calls, partly because he thought it impolite to do anything else, partly because he found endless pleasure in observing the different manners of the artists. There would be one lady who bowed herself even unto the ground to show her humility and how greatly she valued the good opinion of the audience; and another who only went halfway in order that she could show her delighted surprise. "You are too kind," she seemed to say. "I don't deserve it—truly I do not." And then there was Davie's favourite prima donna who stood erect with a friendly smile and bowed only from the neck, as who should say "How right you are." The final entertainment was the operatic hand-shake when all the singers line up holding hands, and everyone congratulates his neighbours with paralytic little sideways shakes. Davie always enjoyed that part very much. And so the red curtain rose and fell, rose and fell, and nobody in the gallery booed. It had been an excellent evening.

And now the lights were up and Davie nipped out of the theater and made his way to the Strand, passing a group of teenagers outside the Lyceum, hot from their own rhythmical experiences. "One day," thought Davie, "if I can get someone to come with me I'd like to go in there and see what happens. It sounds entertaining—but perhaps a little too easy to do. When I think of all those dancing lessons we had when we were small . . ."

In the Strand he hopped on a No. 15 which took him to Piccadilly Circus. It was a short walk from there to the Chesterfield.

Alfred, the second hall porter, let him in. From the room on the left came a murmur of voices, but Davie was not in need of company. He went straight up to his room. He was tired and did not even mean to read in bed.

No one had drawn his curtains, he noticed. One never got quite the same service nowadays, not even at the Chesterfield. He crossed to the window, drew aside the net and looked out. The moon was full in his face, just risen above the dark cliffs of the houses opposite. It shone on the unexpected little garden and made fantastic shadows from the branches of the catalpa tree. On that side criss-crossed like a harp, on the other thick and splayed like a man's legs.

He pulled the curtains and got into bed.

Before he put the light out he tried, as he had often tried before, to work out the geography of the wallpaper. There was a boy fishing in a river and further along another boy, also fishing. Davie liked to suppose that it was the same river, in which case the elegant ladies sitting by a haycock were in a field near the bank. But, if that were so, the church and the market-square . . . Perhaps it did not admit a solution, but he always tried to find it.

He snipped out the light and closed his eyes. There was no time to lose. "The huntsmen are up in America," he repeated, "and they are already past their first sleep in Persia." Very contentedly he crossed the frontier.

3

I

"Aurora spread her rosy mantle," said Davie to himself when he woke up at six-thirty. It was one of Lord Chesterfield's advices to his son. "In prose," the old dandy had written, "you would say 'the beginning of the morning or the break of day'; but that would not do in verse; and you must rather say 'Aurora spread her rosy mantle.' " Davie lay there thinking about the unfortunate young man, who had been told among other things never to laugh—"there is nothing so illiberal, and so ill bred as audible laughter": and never to participate in music—"it puts a gentleman in a very frivolous and contemptible light." He hoped the young man had been too nitwitted to take much notice.

And then it was seven o'clock and in came Henry, the valet, to draw the curtains, deposit a tea tray, and deliver his morning bulletin about the weather, which he always did very fast and in an almost unintelligible North Country accent. Davie gathered it was fine at the moment but likely to rain any time now. And then Henry was off. He had to tell a good many other gentlemen about the weather.

Davie never lingered in bed after drinking his tea. He was shaving at twenty past seven. He was out of his bath by a quarter to eight. Then, trousered but as yet without his tie, he strolled across to the window and (wondering how Aurora was getting on outside) lifted the net curtain. No shadows like a harp lay interlaced upon the grass: but the shadows like the legs of a man had not departed. They *were* the legs of a man and presumably they had been there all night.

Davie dropped the net curtain, quickly tied his tie and climbed into his coat. There was nobody about outside. He hurried down the corridor, opened the glass door, crossed the landing, opened the second glass door and walked down the further corridor to the secretary's room.

Captain Blonde opened his door immediately. He was already dressed. "Hullo, Davie," he said. "What can I do for you at this early hour?"

"There's something wrong in the garden," Davie began.

"Something wrong?"

"There's a man lying there."

"A man?" said Blonde, wrinkling his eyebrows. "What do you mean? Show me."

He strode across his room to the window.

"By the gazebo," said Davie, following him. "You can only see his legs."

"I don't see anything."

"Sorry. He's the other side. I was forgetting: the gazebo's in the way."

Captain Blonde was not the sort of man to waste time talking. He opened the window and stepped onto the fire escape. "Come on," he said; "it's quicker this way and we shan't meet anyone."

The head and shoulders rested on the floor of the gazebo; the rest of the body lay on the grass. The black hair was not untidy. The blue eyes were open. He looked alive, but like a man horribly paralyzed.

"Morris Brent," whispered Davie.

Blonde stooped down and touched his hand. "Dead cold," he said. "Stiff."

"I thought so," said Davie. "I think he's been there all night. Don't move him."

"I know the rules," said Blonde. "Come on—let's get back. I'll have to telephone the police. I'll go up first if I may."

"Certainly," said Davie. "You're much quicker on your pins than I am."

Five minutes later, standing by the window of Blonde's room and staring down at the garden, Davie said, "I know it's inappropriate to say so— but lying there like that under the catalpa tree early in the morning he looked like an illustration to Blake's poem—

In the morning glad I see
My foe outstretch'd beneath the tree."

Captain Blonde was not a student of William Blake. He looked at Davie gravely. "Whose foe was Brent?" he asked.

"Nobody's that I know. I said my remark was inappropriate. It was just the picture. It might have been done by one of the pre-Raphaelites, every grain of wood, every plantain, every daffodil, every button carefully delineated."

"H'm," said Blonde.

"Still—he must have been somebody's foe," said Davie quietly. "He'd been hit in the face: there was a bruise by his left eye."

52

The telephone rang. It was Alfred speaking from the hall. "Some gentlemen to see you, sir. Is it too early, or—"

"Show them into the billiards room," said Captain Blonde. "I'll be down immediately."

"Very good, sir."

"You must come too, Davie. They'll want to know everything we can tell them. I said the billiards room because that's bound to be empty."

As they left the room Davie noticed the first drops of water trickling down the windowpane. Henry's weather prediction had been precisely right. Besides being unpleasant, he reflected, it was going to be increasingly difficult to find any clues there might have been in the garden. Already the one small evidence that he had noticed would almost certainly have disappeared.

II

Chief Inspector Mays recognized Davie immediately.

"You know each other?" said Blonde.

"Yes, sir: Dr. Davie helped us over a case last year. He had committed a burglary—"

"Eh?" said Blonde.

"But in a good cause, Blonde, I assure you."

"And what has happened here, gentlemen?"

"You begin, Davie," said Blonde.

"May I suggest you take the officers into the garden before this light rain turns to something worse," said Davie.

"In the garden, is it?" said Mays. "Certainly. Let's go at once."

"There will be people in the dining room by this time," said Blonde. "We must just troop through as though we were going to look at the outside plumbing."

The rain had in fact stalled for a little. Davie followed the party into the garden and, standing by the gazebo, he told Mays how he had seen the body lying there on the previous night and had thought it a shadow of the tree, and how he had discovered the truth in the morning.

"The only people who have been out here are Dr. Davie and myself," Blonde said. "We didn't stay more than a minute and we moved nothing."

"Good," said Mays.

"There's nothing I can do, I think," said Davie, "and it's rather cold. Shall I go back to your room, Blonde, and wait for you?"

"Yes, do."

"I shan't be long," said Mays. "The others can get on with it while I'm talking to you gentlemen."

So Davie walked across to the fire escape. It was a pretty little spiral affair, newly painted green, admirably suited to the house. Fresh washed by the rain, it shone in the returning sunlight. It was the steepest but the shortest way up, and as he did not want to walk through the dining room Davie decided to use it. For the second time that day he plodded up the turning stairs. And when he reached the secretary's room he was glad to flop into an armchair.

He had never been in the secretary's room before and for a moment he glanced about him. Blonde was comfortably housed. On the dressing table were good ivory-backed brushes. The swivel glass looked genuine Queen Anne. There was a splendid tallboy. A marquetry table stood against the wall. Above it hung a painting: French surely—it looked like a Bonnard. The room was more like an important bedroom in a country house. On the table were magazines which had evidently come up from the club rooms on the arrival of new issues—Blackwood's, The Field, Country Life, Plays and Players, Opera, The London Magazine, The Cornhill.

Sitting there waiting, Davie ran over in his mind the troubles and puzzles that lay ahead. The field of investigation was limited by the club membership and the staff: but it was, nevertheless, a large field. A good many members had had lunch at the club yesterday. Picturing the tables in his mind he reckoned they might have been about seventy. Miss Mittens kept a list. They would all be identified. There would be a few others who had visited the club in the afternoon. Craddock would remember most of them. He would miss some, but they would probably identify themselves. And then there would be the diners. Nearly all would be able to prove exactly where they had been all the afternoon and evening. But there would be a few gaps of an unsuspicious character. For instance Davie himself had been seen by Dyke and Dyke had been seen by Davie at two-forty-five: but Davie certainly, and Dyke probably, had been seen by no one else until after four-thirty.

The corridor leading from the hall to the dining room led also to the cloakroom. And you could reach the cloakroom by the second door in the morning room and from the bedrooms by the back stairs. Anyone visiting the cloakroom could have gone into the dining room instead, and so to the garden. The hall porter was not in a position to see. Nor was he likely to remember if anyone was absent in that direction longer than usual. Besides why should anyone be absent longer than usual? It takes no longer to knock a man cold than it does to visit the Gents. At which point Davie perceived that he was anticipating. Perhaps the doctor would report a thrombosis. Perhaps Brent had hit himself in falling. Perhaps: but Davie did not think so, not for a moment. Some time between three and shortly after eleven o'clock (when Davie had looked out of his window) someone had done Brent in.

III

Davie had been left alone with Mays. There was a great deal at the moment to occupy Captain Blonde. Mays would have to interview every-one and everyone was by no means available. The staff were the easiest people to find. Meantime there was Davie.

There was not much to tell. At least seventy people besides himself could witness that Brent had been well and in good spirits at luncheon. After luncheon Brent had gone to the billiards room. Davie had also been there for a few minutes before going upstairs. Like himself, Brent had been watching, not playing. And (now Davie thought about it) he had been rather restless. He had not kept his seat long, and at one time had stared out of the window instead of following the game. He left the room soon after—at about twenty to three. Davie didn't know where he had gone. He himself had gone upstairs at two-forty-five, and had seen Dyke in the library. Apart from that Davie could only tell how he had almost certainly seen Brent when he looked out of his window before going to bed—a shadow beneath the catalpa tree like the legs of a man.

"Sometime between three and eleven," said Mays. "It's a wide gap."

"But I suppose the doctor can narrow it," said Davie; and as the policeman said no more, he added "Will it be all right for me to go back to Cambridge?"

"Yes, sir—but you'll be needed for the inquest."

"When?"

"I would think the day after tomorrow."

"I'll be back tomorrow afternoon," said Davie, half rising in his seat, but Mays asked, "Would you wait a few minutes, sir, till Captain Blonde gets back? You might be able to help me with some members of the staff."

There was a knock at the door.

"The Captain says you would like to see me, sir," said old Craddock.

"This is our hall porter, Inspector," said Davie. "Mr. Craddock."

It had been a quiet afternoon according to Craddock—after the members had gone off after luncheon. He remembered Mr. Robbin going out late, a little before three o'clock. "He came out from the cloakroom corridor rather fast, like he was late. That's why I remember him," said Craddock. "Dr. Marchant went out soon after." Craddock smiled at the police officer. He was rather proud to be interrogated on matters concerning his office. "Sir Matthew," he said, "come in about half past three."

"Matthew Werner," Davie put in.

"And Sir Matthew asked for Mr. Brent—as he had, come to think of it, in the morning. He was expecting him because he come out into the hall twice from the morning room to ask if he'd come in, but he hadn't, and so of course I said No, Sir Matthew, he has not come in I said. And what's more, I said, I don't think he ever went out. He's here somewhere, I said." Craddock paused and rubbed the end of his nose very hard. He seemed to suggest that he had dealt with Sir Matthew rather well. Then he added "There was a lady rang Mr. Brent several times."

"You said Sir Matthew Werner came in about three-thirty."

"Yes, sir."

"And you also said he'd been in in the morning."

"Yes, sir."

"Then when did he go out? Was he here for lunch?"

"No, sir. He come down at about a quarter to one. He went out just as most of the gentlemen was coming in."

"I remember hearing him say he wouldn't be in for lunch," said Davie in parenthesis.

Mays made a note. Then, "Are you alone when you are on duty in the hall?" he asked.

"Yes, sir."

"Do you have to answer outside calls on the telephone?"

This was Craddock's familiar grievance. "Yes, sir. It's going all the time, proper nuisance it is. The board's behind my desk."

"And you switch the calls through to one of the boxes, I suppose, and inform the member concerned."

"Yes, sir, that is how we do it."

"So you can't always keep note of everyone who comes in and out."

"I do the best I can, sir."

"I'm sure you do—but sometimes you'd be turned round to the board—and sometimes, I suppose, you'd be looking in one of the rooms for a member?"

"Yes, sir. It's one person's work. There used to be a page boy one time, didn't there, Dr. Davie, but it's all different these days, and it's getting too much for me. I told Captain Blonde."

"Do you remember if you had to be absent much between say two and three o'clock?"

"Yes, sir, I did that—about five times, and once it was upstairs in the card room."

"I see. Anything else you can remember about people coming in or out?"

"Soon after Sir Matthew come in the Captain come in. He stopped in the hall for a word with Mr. Gordon. Mr. Gordon was asking for change for the telephone. I always have some in my drawer. Mr. Gordon was making a lot of calls yesterday."

"Where are the telephones?" asked Mays.

"Down the corridor, opposite the cloaks."

Mays consulted his notes. "Captain Blonde came in a bit after three-thirty then?"

"Yes, sir."

"When did he go out?"

"Before lunch," said Craddock. "About one."

When Craddock had gone Davie said, "I remember hearing Brent tell Sir Matthew Werner before lunch that he'd be in all the afternoon. Werner wanted to talk about something."

"Although one would think it must be an inside job," said Mays, "it's obvious that there must have been ample opportunity for anyone to slip in when Craddock was on one of his member-hunting expeditions. One is reminded that Jack Ruby only needed ten unguarded seconds to get into the basement of the Dallas city gaol."

"He didn't get out again," observed Davie.

"True."

"And how would such a person know that Brent was in the garden?"

Mays nodded his head. "H'm," he said.

The next knock was gentle and it announced the presence of Miss Mittens.

"It must have been a quarter to three when I saw Mr. Brent," she said. "I know because I was later than usual and as I went downstairs the hall clock said eleven minutes to."

"Do you wear glasses, Miss Mittens?" asked Mays.

Miss Mittens blushed a delicate pink. One minute earlier, prompted by vanity, she had taken them off and popped them in her bag.

"Not as often as I should. I do have them—for distance, you know. But I don't always wear them."

"Were you wearing them when you looked out of the office window?"

"I really can't remember."

"Are you sure it was Mr. Brent that you saw?"

"Certainly," said Miss Mittens. "It must have been Mr. Brent."

"Why 'must'?"

"Well," said Miss Mittens, as though surprised at the inspector's obtuseness, "it was Mr. Brent who was killed, wasn't it?"

Mays did not pursue the matter.

"What was this person doing?" he asked.

"He was walking across the lawn to the gazebo," said Miss Mittens. "I suppose—" But the inspector was not interested in Miss Mittens's suppositions. He asked her to furnish a list of members who had been present at luncheon; and presently pointed the need for departure by politely opening the door.

"That is something," said Mays. "Someone—and probably it was Mr. Brent—was seen in the garden at a quarter to three. The difficulty will be to find who else thought well to visit the garden on a not very warm afternoon."

"I perceive," said Davie after a pause, "that you do think this is a case of what is strangely described as 'foul play'?"

"I think so," said Mays slowly. "Though there is one odd thing about it. He was hit in the face—but not heavily. He hit his head in falling—but not severely. It doesn't seem enough."

"People have killed themselves before now by tripping over the mat," said Davie.

IV

Cambridge. It was early afternoon when Davie turned out of St. Nicholas Lane and walked down the broad flag-stones of the Long Walk.

At the porter's lodge Mr. Jump raised a stately hand to his hat brim. Beyond the gate tower First Court lay full of sunshine and surrounded by spring flowers. No one was about: but as he passed through the arch into Baxter's Court, sounds from the Close announced that lusty young men were tearing about on the football field—an exercise which Davie had abandoned with relief immediately he had been released from the bonds of school. He had never taken any exercise since—except fives (which is the deepest exercise of all): and he had not played fives for forty years. He had done very well without exercise: and indeed was disposed to believe that lazy people lived longer than athletic ones.

Davie climbed the steps of M staircase and let himself into his rooms. Through the open door of the sitting room he could see his letters, neatly disposed on the table by Mrs. Tibbs, the bed-maker: but he was not going to investigate them before he had visited the gyp room and put on the kettle. Tea: after a little reflection he decided that the needs of the day would be best satisfied with two spoons of Jasmine and one of Lapsang Suchong. Then he carried his tray to the table in the window, got a box of Bourbon biscuits out of a cupboard, picked up his mail, and sat down. A bill, a bill, a bill, an invitation to a College Feast (good: Davie enjoyed Feasts)—here he poured out the tea—an invitation to give away the prizes at a girls' school (bad. Davie hated making allegedly impromptu speeches), a letter from New Zealand, a letter from America (Davie was a great one for keeping up with old pupils and itinerant nephews), a bill, an advertisement for a concert, and a packet from—where? Davie squinted at the postmark. It was illegible. He opened the wrappers. Inside was a small flat box similar to the one he already had in his bag: and a note from Miss Cragg.

Dear Dr. Davie—

Here is the promised tape. I am sorry I could not give it to you this morning. We are making the next part of the course on March 10. I wish you could be there.

We all enjoyed your lecture.

Mary Clegg

Davie, who was childishly fond of parcels, was disappointed. Just another tape: presumably the efficient Miss Cragg had whipped it off before Miss Eggar had had time to tell her not to bother. In the circumstances he felt justified in taking another Bourbon biscuit.

But, nevertheless, half an hour later Davie took the tape out of his box and fitted it on his machine. He did this partly because of his genuine interest in the uses of English, but mostly because of a sense of good manners towards Miss Cragg. She had taken the trouble to send it. He did not wish to reject her amiable advances. And so for the second time in two days he heard the young man gallantly declare that he would like to take the young lady to the theater again, and "Thank you," said the young lady. "That would be delightful." "I shall look forward to that," said the young man.

It made a proper ending, and for a few seconds Davie did not remember that anything was missing. And then suddenly he said to himself, "What's happened to 'La donna e mobile'? And surely there was a definite date for the party?"

He fetched Miss Eggar's tape—and there of course it was: "I shall be free on Wednesday the fourth." "I shall look forward to that," and then "La donna è mobile." It had sounded a bit odd before: that was why Brent had gone back on it and played it again: but now, in comparison with Miss Cragg's tape it seemed absurdly clumsy. "How peculiar!" Davie was thinking, and automatically he put his hand in his pocket and fished out his engagement book. Vaguely he was wondering whether such a date as Wednesday the fourth existed. In the front of the book were calendars for 1966 and 1967. He ran his eye over them. May 4, 1966 had been a Wednesday. Nothing else in 1966. In 1967 there was January 4, recently past, and October 4 in the future. Turning over a few pages he came to January 4 and his own engagements. Yes—he had been staying at the Gainsborough: he had lunched with George Canteloupe in the City and he'd been to Covent Garden to hear Cornell MacNeil in *Rigo-letto*, with the admirable Aragall and the wholly enchanting Reri Grist—and that's odd, thought Davie suddenly: "I shall be free on Wednesday the fourth"—followed by "La donna è mobile." It's almost a private appointment—rather skittishly made. If that's Willy Marchant's idea of a joke it's ponderously obscure. But then, he thought, Miss Cragg's tape must be the true text, in which case . . . In which case the other one's been altered. Altered by editing. He took a look at it. There was nothing to show—which meant, of course, that it was a clean copy of an edited tape. No doubt there had been other copies and presumably they had been sent somewhere or other. It was no business of his, but it did seem an odd thing to bother to do.

Davie was early to bed that night. He was tired, but the moment he snipped his bedside light out he felt widely awake and ready to think. In the morning he had very calmly accepted that Brent had probably been murdered. But was that likely? Who could be his foe? Brent was evidently going around with Lady Werner—but did educated people commit crimes of passion in England? Certainly there had been a tension between Brent and Werner, but Brent had showed no signs of worry when he had been listening with Davie to Willy Marchant's tape, only a few hours before his death.

Willy Marchant's tape, with its comic ending: he did not know why he should worry his head with it. Maybe the director had made one version—not liked it—and then, more soberly, produced another. It was an easy and possible answer—but it ignored the coincidence of the date. Davie was fascinated by that date. There must be a more certain explanation, just as there had to be an explanation for the disappearance of the cucumber. Miss Murchiston, Davie reflected, had successfully solved her problem, and why shouldn't he? It would be no use asking silly Willy. If it had been done without his knowledge he wouldn't have the answer: and Davie had no intention of stirring up trouble between Willy and St. Martha's. But someone had altered the tape and for a reason. Davie found himself wondering if the reason could have been a bad reason. And as he thought about it, he saw, not himself listening to the tape in Cambridge, but Morris Brent listening to it in London—listening and going back on it and listening again.

Davie did not complete the thought because at that point he suddenly went to sleep. But when he awoke at six-thirty he went straight on from where he had left off. A long time he lay in bed, pondering on Willy Marchant's English course, and when he had come to some sort of conclusion he got up, dressed, and, as soon as a civilized person could do such a thing, he telephoned to Miss Eggar. He thought he would like to accept Miss Cragg's kind invitation to watch the new tape being made. But for reasons which he would explain when he got there he thought it would be best if Miss Eggar did not announce the fact.

"Do come," said Miss Eggar. "They start at ten-thirty. Don't you think you had better come the night before?"

"I shall be in London," said Davie, "so it won't be a long journey. I think I'd rather come on the day of the recording. But I have an idea that I might do well to stay the following night. May I do that?"

"Goodness, yes," said Miss Eggar. "If you'll promise to tell me why."

"I will, indeed," said Davie—"when I see you."

"That will be the train getting here at nine-thirty-five," said Miss Eggar. "I'll meet you."

Admirable woman, thought Davie: no fuss, no questions. He looked at his watch. It was a quarter past nine. He had to attend a committee at ten-thirty (that was why he had come back to Cambridge). There was time then to fill in his opera book. And when he had written down his notes on the night before last he turned back to look at Wednesday, January 4, the date which had begun to interest him so greatly. There was a full note on an excellent performance. But not much about the audience. Mildred Meade-Fuller had been there, as surprised as ever. And Dyke. And, unexpectedly, Willy Marchant. Davie had forgotten him: but it was embarrassingly easy to forget Willy Marchant.

Davie closed his opera book and watched a shaft of sunlight falling on Letty, his favourite Rockingham Cow, and on the shelf below, on Weekley's *Etymological Dictionary of Modern English*. And that reminded him of "boon companion". He got up from his table, took down Weekley from the shelf, and carried him over to the armchair by the window.

It was disappointing and a little shaming to find that "boon" was only the French "bon", a good companion. He should have known. But why say "boon" if you might say "good"? Language has exquisite undertones. The fact was that one said "boon" (if one did say it) in inverted commas. The word did have a derogatory sort of implication.

It is, of course, fatal to pick up Weekley. Davie could never put him down. With the greatest pleasure he went on to read about "boor", "boost" (origin unknown—how odd!), "booze", and "bosky"—secondary meaning "intoxicated": "may be perverted from Sp. *boquiseco*, dry mouthed, but adjs expressive of drunkenness seem to be created spontaneously (cf. *squiffy*, etc.)." He had just discovered that a brocket was a stag in its second year when muffled sounds in the gyp room betrayed the morning presence of Mrs. Tibbs. Davie opened his door.

"I'm back, Mrs. Tibbs," he said.

"And I hope you had a pleasant visit, sir," said Mrs. Tibbs.

Pleasant was perhaps not the exact word, but Davie said yes, he had, and Mrs. Tibbs said a holiday was good for everyone and that all work and no play made Jack a dull boy, as her poor husband always used to say.

"I'm afraid I take rather more than my share of play these days, Mrs. Tibbs," said Davie.

"Ah," said Mrs. Tibbs, "you've earned it, Dr. Davie. We need a bit of pleasure as our time draws on."

"Well, yes, I suppose we do," said Davie. Like Richard II, Mrs. Tibbs was much given to talking of graves and epitaphs. It was a subject he found uncongenial. So, "I'm off again this afternoon," he said. "Just for a night or two. And now I'm going to have a look at the daffodils in the Close."

"They're a picture, sir," said Mrs. Tibbs.

VI

"Well, Dr. Davie, you are a stranger," said Miss Mercer.

Back in London, Davie had decided to stay at the Gainsborough Hotel, his haunt in Bloomsbury. He did not feel like sleeping at the Chesterfield just now.

"Your room is quite ready," said Miss Mercer. "I saw it this morning—new paper and everything."

"I hope it's not been jazzed up with squares and triangles."

"No, it hasn't. I asked Mr. Delgardo to make it old-fashioned. It's rose-buds and blue ribbons."

"Pale blue, I hope."

"Naturally, Dr. Davie."

"I'm sure I shall like it. It will remind me of my childhood, when bed-steads were brass and had to be polished and had little knobs on them which you could unscrew."

"What memories you have!" said Miss Mercer. "You ought to write a book about it, you really should. Jack, here's Dr. Davie. His usual room."

Jack, with his fabulous smile, conveyed him to the lift.

Davie did not go out again. He had things to think about, notes to make. And the inquest was at ten in the morning. He wouldn't have to say much. But he wouldn't be at ease till it was over.

4

I

It is only the easy and satisfactory inquest that is comfortably completed at a sitting. Davie had felt sure that the inquest on Morris Brent would be adjourned. A man's face does not necessarily admit to the poison that lies within him. A man's body does not necessarily betray the internal hemorrhage that has drained his life away. Morris Brent had suffered a blow and a bump on the head. It needed a post mortem examination to show that there had been another cause of death. Owing to the stoppage of circulation, the pathologist explained, the right side of the heart, the large veins, and the pulmonary artery were distended, the normal indications of suffocation. There were no signs of struggle, such as pressure on the mouth or the throat. There had been no need for such measures. It is not difficult to suffocate an unconscious man. But the internal results of suffocation are not to be disguised. In the opinion of the doctor the deceased had been suffocated at some time after being knocked unconscious.

Then the coroner adjourned the proceedings for a fortnight.

Davie had a word with Mays outside the court. "How are you getting on with all those people?" he asked.

"We've seen the lot," said Mays, "—except one. Mr. Robbin hasn't turned up. You may recall he was one of the members mentioned by Craddock. He'd left the club in a hurry at about three o'clock. He's not at his Somerset address. I believe he's a friend of yours."

"I don't know a thing," said Davie. "But I do know *him*—very well. He's an odd man and goes off suddenly. Sometimes one doesn't hear of him for months."

"We've got to hear of him a lot sooner than that," said Mays. "It's obvious that Brent was killed early. People were telephoning and asking for him all the afternoon. He could never be found. The people I'm interested in are the people who were in the club between two-forty-five and three-thirty. We've got to find Mr. Robbin."

After lunch Davie made his way to the Chesterfield. George Canteloupe was just coming out.

"I say, Canteloupe—before you go, please tell me something. The other day when we were speaking of Morris Brent, you said you'd as soon hobnob with a retired policeman as with an active city gent."

"True."

"And when I said, 'We see your point,' you answered 'You don't—not all of it'."

"Take a turn up the street," said Canteloupe.

"Well—what did you mean? I've been wondering. You said 'I won't elaborate here': elaborate now."

"I meant that there had been a number of members who were not in favour of letting him in. I believe the secretary didn't think it a very good idea. Nor did Willy Marchant and Conway Gordon. Once a policeman, always a policeman. You know."

"Certainly I know. I remember the election of a clergyman being opposed here on the ground that members might have to restrain their language and opinions. It didn't of course occur to the complacent objector that a little restraint of his language and opinions would be welcome anyhow."

"Well—that's how it was," said Canteloupe. "But the objectors weren't on the committee: Matthew Werner was."

"What a good thing!" said Davie. "I suppose the objectors thought Brent was going to follow them about with a magnifying glass and a tape measure. Asses!"

"I agree," said Canteloupe. "Dolts! You're going in. I'm going out. Goodbye."

Davie settled himself down in the morning room. Presently Willy Marchant came in, prancing a little to conceal his accustomed self-consciousness.

"I listened to your tape," said Davie.

Dr. Marchant coloured faintly. His days were full of anxiety. In his official life he was usually in the company of second rate people and there he shone. It was no true pleasure to him to venture into the company of wits and scholars: and yet he felt it was his right and his duty to do so. He was proud of belonging to the Chesterfield, but he half dreaded going there: he was one of those who had never recovered from his fear of the club's reputation for "brilliant" conversation. He expected criticism in advance and the least word of it was going to upset him.

Davie said, "It's very good. I'm sure a foreigner could learn a lot from it. I don't know that anyone ever talks in that way—"

"Oh—don't you think so?" said Dr. Marchant, instantly on the alert.

"No," said Davie. "Nobody talks so accurately."

"Ah," said Willy, relieved.

"It's absurd but true that we have to learn correct speech before we are privileged to indulge in our accustomed jargon."

There were two questions that Davie wanted to ask, and now he produced the first. "I suppose these tapes all go to people abroad?"

"Nearly all," said Willy. "Indeed, it may be all. That's the idea. When you've got the language all round you, you don't need to listen to tapes."

"That's what I supposed."

Then Davie asked the second question. "Are the lessons in the course all on the same lines? Or do you sometimes kick up your heels and introduce music?"

"Goodness, no—no music! It would take up space—and, besides that, there'd be all that awful copyright. You can't just pinch a bit of a music recording, you know. You've got to pay for it."

Willy Marchant was looking pleased. He had been able to talk in an authoritative and informative way to someone who was normally well-informed. He got up and rang the bell with a certain air, and when the waiter came in he ordered tea with a synthetic graciousness that Davie found infinitely entertaining. Then, anxious to maintain a well-won position, he retired behind the defences of *The New Statesman*, where he carried out a number of exercises with his eyebrows and facial muscles intended to denote an intelligent interest in what he was reading. It was not nature but second nature that had trained him in these almost but not quite subconscious performances.

Dr. Marchant finished his tea, looked at his watch with simulated alarm, and rose to go.

"Goodness!" he said. "I must be off or I shall catch it."

This was one of Dr. Marchant's familiar fantasies. He had a neat little house in Ealing with a neat little garden and an obedient wife attentive to all his desires, in the execution of which she had presented him with five daughters. Willy Marchant might easily have been married to a battle-axe. But he had been lucky. Everything at Ealing was sacrificed to father's comfort. Even the neighbours contributed their incense. They were proud to be friends of the eminent educational authority. So when he said "I must be off or I shall catch it", Dr. Marchant had two thoughts in his mind, the first to give his accustomed performance as the jovial and lovable family man, the second to take immediate steps towards a first-class dinner. And if it were not a first-class dinner he would have no hesitation in saying so with no joviality at all. Where he felt safe to tread Willy Marchant trod heavily.

"Good night," said Davie.

Captain Blonde came in. "It's all in the *Standard,*" he said.

"Of course," said Davie. "It must be very frustrating for them not to be able to say more."

"A photographer fellow got on top of one of the houses in Bullivant Mews and took a picture of the garden."

"That was to be expected."

"And there are two reporters outside the door."

"That also."

"Are you staying the night?"

"Not here," said Davie, "I'm passing through."

Captain Blonde, elbows on knees and staring at the carpet, was not really interested in Davie's movements. "Do you know anything about Robbin?" he asked.

"Not a thing," said Davie. "I gather they can't find him."

"Yes."

"He often disappears, you know. He's got nothing to tie him. He likes to dash off whenever he feels like it."

"It's an awkward moment to do it."

"Very. He'll turn up when he knows he's needed. But if he's gone abroad that may not be at once."

"You were lunching with him two days ago. Did he say anything about going away?"

"No—he didn't."

"I wish he'd turn up," said Blonde.

Then, "Werner's very upset," he added. "It appears Brent was having an affair with his wife."

"Yes, I knew that."

"You did? Apparently Werner was looking for Brent that very afternoon in order to have it out with him. He admits it."

"Careful!" said Davie. Through the window he had just seen Matthew Werner mounting the club steps, holding a newspaper between his face and the camera man who had been waiting for this opportunity all day. The man even laid a hand on Werner's sleeve and tried to detain him.

Half a minute later Werner entered the room.

"Hullo," said Blonde. "How's things?" It sounded embarrassed. He felt embarrassed.

"Pretty uncomfortable, thanks," said Werner. "You needn't put on any pretenses. I know. I'm news. It's an extraordinary thing—while Brent was alive the fact that he was tagging after my wife may have been known, but it wasn't considered interesting. Now that the poor chap's dead it suddenly becomes absorbingly important. I've been dodging reporters and photographers all day, besides answering questions from the police. Believe me, if I'd gone out for a solitary walk between one and half past three that afternoon I'd have been in an awkward position. But fortunately I had lunch at Berto's. And after I'd left the place I had to go back for a book."

"Oh," said Blonde. "Good. That's very fortunate."

Werner rang a bell and sank down wearily in a deep chair. For a few seconds nobody spoke. Then "Did you get your book?" said Davie.

"What book?" said Werner.

"The one you left at Berto's."

"Oh, that—no, I didn't. Somebody'd pinched it. In the matter of books the dishonesty of even the most respectable people is incredible."

"I agree. By the way, I ought to introduce myself. I know who you are, but you don't know me. My name's Davie."

"I know you well enough by sight," said Werner. "I've seen you sometimes at the opera."

"I dare say you have. It's a great place for picking up faces. Some people there I've silently known for years. I'm sorry you're having so much trouble. It must be infinitely wearing."

"My God, it is," said Werner.

And then Conway Gordon came in, followed by the waiter.

"A double brandy and a small ginger ale, please," said Werner.

"Yes, Sir Matthew."

"Going to Covent Garden, Davie?" said Gordon. "You usually are."

"No," said Davie. "It doesn't seem the right night."

"It's never the right night for me," said Gordon. "It's a diversion I don't understand."

"You play bridge," said Davie, "and I don't understand that. Forty years ago, in the days of auction, I played quite a bit—but I never learnt the new rules. One must not, I believe, kick one's partner under the table or pass him a note, but there seems to be a sort of code whereby you convey the information nonetheless. One says three diamonds over two clubs and one's partner immediately divines by preconcerted plan that one has the ace of hearts. Do you deny it?"

"Certainly."

"I felt sure you would. I told you I didn't understand. But that's how it looks to me when I read those fascinating columns by the experts who never make a mistake of any sort, and work unashamedly on a sort of verbal semaphore. And now before you start contradicting me, which is a thing I cannot abide, I really must go. I leave you, not without misgiving, to those graceless diversions which a gentleman's club so lavishly affords. I am going out to dinner."

He was in fact going back to the Gainsborough to dine on a predictable menu of clear soup, suprême of chicken, and a choice of trifle, poire Hélène, and ices various. It would be dull but good. The Gainsborough in its own way was very good.

"How old Davie talks!" said Conway Gordon, settling himself into his usual chair.

"Yes," said Matthew Werner. "He's good, isn't he?"

But that was not what Conway Gordon had meant.

II

There was too much noise in the bar. Davie peeped into the drawing-room. The lights were out. Seven dowagers, two men, and a child, were solemnly watching an advertisement for a soap that made your clothes whiter. ("Whiter than what?" Davie asked himself. "That's what they never say.") Then the subject changed and a man and a girl in close harmony commended somebody's chocolates very warmly indeed. Then a teen-ager was shown swallowing an aerated drink at a party. "It's gorgeous!" she said. "It's Bippo!" Davie withdrew.

The quietest place proved to be that room which is strangely denominated the lounge. No one was lounging. No one had his feet on the sofa. No one was lying on the floor. Indeed there was only one man in the room and he was sitting bolt upright on a hard chair reading an evening paper. Davie crossed the room to an armchair by a curtained window in the corner, and sat there for two or three minutes quite still, contemplating the ingenuities of the carpet, which interwove the monogram GH with an interminable vista of pink roses wreathed with ivy. Even a carpet pattern had a clue, he was thinking. Did the design start with three rose-buds and work upwards, or were the rosebuds the apex of a design which had begun lower down with the ivy leaves? It was as baffling as the toile de Jouy paper.

Presently he drew a small notebook from his pocket. On yesterday's journey from Cambridge he had filled several pages with his thoughts and questions about the Willy Marchant tape. Last night he had summarized the notes. Now, he wondered, would they still make sense?

1. The tape with music has not followed Willy Marchant's text. There must be a reason for this, because there is another tape which does follow it.
2. Either Marchant does not know about the tape with music (which seems probable), or conceivably he does know, but assumes that I do not.
3. The tape with music could be merely an experiment by the director, afterwards abandoned in favour of the plain version.

   This seems improbable. The work was jaggedly done—as though perfection were not necessary—as though it would sound all right to the right ears. Besides, the tape with music refers to a particular day, and possibly refers to a particular occasion. It sounds like a coded appointment.

Under this Davie had drawn a line. Beneath the line he had written:

This certainly is no business of mine. But there is something odd about it. Simple enquiries may resolve the whole thing. But if they don't there may be some good in my curiosity.

Before going to bed Davie looked into the drawing-room again. The same dedicated group were still sitting there, but two of the dowagers had dropped asleep. He watched the last minutes of a film about a cowboy and a crooked sheriff. It was followed by the picture of the girl at the party drinking the aerated drink. "It's gorgeous!" she said. "It's Bippo!"

"That girl will do herself an injury if she's not careful," thought Davie as he closed the drawing room door.

After saying goodnight to Miss Mercer he made his way upstairs. In the subdued light of the bedside lamp the rose-buds and the light blue ribbons were certainly attractive. There had been a paper like it in his aunt's house near Seaton. At least sixty years ago. On the mantelpiece there had been a china monkey that nodded its head and had both fascinated and frightened him when he was very small. He could also remember crying—aged three—on being put into his aunt's brassy motorcar. That he could ever have been such a fool was even now a matter for regret. Then he thought with pleasure of the red japonica by the front door steps, the first exquisitely beautiful thing in his memory. Then he recalled his aunt's gramophone which played cylindrical records.

No doubt this freshet of nostalgia justly arose from the bedroom wallpaper. But subconsciously Davie had perhaps hoped to get to sleep without thinking about Morris Brent. It was no good. The ancient cylinders reminded him of the modern tape and the tape reminded him of Brent, and there he was thinking of Matthew Werner and his cause for offense; and of Robbin who had inconveniently disappeared. But what could Robbin have to do with it? He had had to ask who Brent was that day at luncheon. And Werner—these days English husbands, regardless of honour, were usually only too glad to have a clear excuse for getting rid of a flighty wife. To Davie the two obvious candidates for the murder of Morris Brent were—on the face of it—totally improbable. The only argument against Robbin was that he had gone away in a hurry. If he came back he would appear no more probable a criminal than Willy Marchant, or Dyke, or Conway Gordon, or himself for that matter.

And at that point Davie drew a mental line. He was not, repeat not, investigating the death of Morris Brent. It was nothing to do with him. His very much smaller interest lay in Willy Marchant's tape. Let it stay there.

He had that afternoon in a small bookseller's shop picked up a pretty copy of Mrs. Trollope's famous work *Domestic Manners of the Americans*. He opened it now. "On the 4th November, 1827," he began, "I sailed from London, accompanied by my son and two daughters; and after a favourable, though somewhat tedious voyage, arrived on Christmas-day at the mouth of the Mississippi."

It was the perfect antidote. Far into the night he read this remarkable book. And when he was tired he went to sleep untroubled.

5

I

Miss Eggar drove Davie up to the new buildings and set him down by the door nearest the studio.

"Come to the Lodge when you've finished," she said. "We'll have lunch."

"Thank you very much," said Davie, "I will—and thanks for meeting me."

He knew his way. Outside the studio he paused to look through the small window in the door. They were already at work. Away to the left George Tallent was sitting by his recording machinery. In the center Mary Cragg, her back towards the door, sat facing a large glass panel looking into the studio beyond. She was in the act of consulting a stop-watch and making pencil notes on a large writing pad.

Beyond the glass panel, in the studio itself, standing on either side of a suspended microphone, was a young man and a young woman. The young man, good-looking in an epicene way, was no doubt the actor hired for the occasion. The young woman was Daphne Maiden.

Davie opened the door gently. George Tallent, his fingers on the intercom switch, was saying, "Turn your head slightly when you say 'Hullo!', Andrew." Then Mary Cragg said, "I've got two points. Daphne—line 14— 'far as'—it's coming over 'far ras'. Red rag to Dr. Marchant's bull: and I don't like it either."

"Nor do I," said Davie, "if I dare say so."

Mary Cragg swung around in her chair.

"Dr. Davie! How kind of you to come!"

"Not a bit. Thank you for asking me."

"Here's a chair, Dr. Davie," said George Tallent.

"We're rehearsing."

"I see you are. Please go on. That's what I've come to see."

Miss Cragg returned to the intercom.

"The other thing was—um—oh yes—Andrew—I thought it was a mistake at first, but you've twice said 'beautiful' in a rather prissy way. The

72

proper English way is to accent the first syllable and let the rest take their chance."

Andrew held up his hand. "Point taken," he said.

"I think that's all," said Miss Cragg. "Let's have a go. We'll have to do it twice, as well you know. But if you're good it's in the bag."

"In the bag" sounded good to Davie. She might so easily have said "we shall have completed our assignment." He decided he was in favour of Miss Cragg; and (unusually for him) he liked her well-creased brown trousers and the light blue thing she wore on top.

"Stand by," said George Tallent, starting his tape. Then he announced "English Conversation Course Number Seven. Take One."

A green cue light flashed. On the other side of the glass panel the duologue began.

Davie listened carefully: he was interested in the whole undertaking: but in particular he was waiting for the end.

It appeared that the young couple, regardless of the proprieties, were going on a tour in a car. Today they were in Cambridge, looking at King's Chapel. Presently Andrew said "We must be going." "I would like to come back," said Daphne. "It is so beautiful." "Right," said Andrew. "We can do that on the way home."

"Thank you," said Mary Cragg. "Half a minute till George is ready and we'll do it again. I haven't any notes. 'Far as' was right, Daphne."

"And that's how you end?" asked Davie. "No signature tunes or such-like draperies."

"No, nothing at all" said Miss Cragg. "It's not meant to be—"

"Dolled up," put in George Tallent.

"And there'd be a lot of work choosing the right music."

"And a lot of getting away without paying for it," said George.

Daphne and Andrew made a second recording.

"What happens now?" asked Davie.

"I've made notes," said Mary Cragg. "There are one or two places where one tape is better than the other. So George does a bit of snipping and joining and we get the best possible performance from the two. If it were something like a poetry reading we might take hours: but this is easy. It won't take us half an hour to get it straight."

Daphne Maiden and Andrew put their heads in at the door.

"Please can we go?" asked Andrew.

"Yes—but first meet Dr. Davie. Dr. Davie, this is Andrew Wynne."

"The hero of Dr. Marchant's serial thriller," said Andrew.

Davie laughed. "I believe you'd like to have each episode ending like an old Pearl White film," he said.

"Who was Pearl White?" asked Daphne.

"Alas! Such is Fame. Pearl White was a heroine of early film serials. She was endlessly pursued by villains and used to be left at the end of each episode hanging over the edge of a precipice or tied to a railway line or falling out of a balloon."

"That's what I meant," said Andrew. "That's just what this series needs—if only Dr. Marchant would see it. We're so wet."

"I won't join in your criticism," said Davie, partly for the benefit of Miss Cragg, who, he suspected, was less light-hearted about her series than the gay Andrew. "You're a very grammatical couple—and that was the idea."

"Of course," said Miss Cragg. "Excuse me a moment. I've got to telephone. I won't be long, George."

"Still—you have a point," said Davie, pursuing the conversation. "I perceive endless possibilities."

"Such as Daphne being lured into a side chapel by the villain disguised as a verger under the pretense of showing her his fan vaulting," said Andrew. "Or it might be better if he were the Dean."

"Oh no, it wouldn't," said Davie. "You mustn't be disrespectful about Deans. And, all things considered, I think you mustn't be disrespectful about Dr. Marchant."

"It was you who brought in Pearl White," said Andrew.

"Was it? I regret it. It was entirely irresponsible. I withdraw."

"How disappointing!" said Andrew.

"Do you live near here, or do you come down specially for this?" asked Davie.

"I come down in my dangerous little car. I live in romantic Chelsea."

"Chelsea? My world exactly. I used to have a minute house near Sloane Square."

"I'm the other end."

"The World's End?"

"Roughly."

Andrew put down his novel, a briefcase, and a script on Mary Cragg's table.

"It's like this," he said, helping himself to a scribbling pad. "Fulham Road—King's Road—and, midway between the two, Elm Park Road. That's me—between The Vale and Beaufort Street."

"I know," said Davie.

Andrew gathered up his things. "Well," he said. 'Can we go or can't we?"

"Yes, you can," said Mary Cragg, coming back into the studio. "Thank you both very much."

"It's all there," said George Tallent.

"Goodbye Dr. Davie," said Daphne.

"Goodbye," said Andrew.

"An engaging couple," said Davie after the door was shut. "How did you find the young man?"

"Dr. Marchant suggested him," said Miss Cragg. "He's adjudicated him at some verse-speaking competition and thought he'd be just right—and so he is."

Davie watched them editing. As he followed George Tallent's nimble fingers he was suddenly reminded of Dr. Marie Baendels and her film editing. She could not possibly have done such delicate work wearing those artificial talons. She must have taken them off, as a woman sheds her rings. It was an appalling thought, an indecency in plastic. Davie shuddered, and hastily switched his mind back to the strong, blunt fingers of George Tallent—and, "There it is," said Tallent, "finished. There wasn't much to do this time."

"Magic," said Davie. "And that is the master copy?"

"Yes."

"And all the tapes you send out are just copies of that?"

"Yes."

"How long does it take to make them?"

"Just so long as it takes to run it through," said Tallent. "I reel them off this afternoon six at a time, and finish tomorrow. It's not a huge assignment."

"No," said Mary Cragg. "We send to certain universities abroad and they send to us. It's an experiment. It's not a commercial enterprise."

"Then your part's finished?" said Davie.

"Except for sending them off. George carries on and makes the tapes. Then I collect them and they're posted. A first batch tomorrow, the rest next day probably."

In the hall outside the studio a grandfather clock chimed one.

"Lunch time," said Miss Cragg, gathering up her scattered papers and stuffing them into her briefcase. Several leaves fluttered to the ground. George and Davie picked them up.

"Confusion!" said Miss Cragg. "So sorry. I have never succeeded in disciplining inanimate objects. For me they fly. Particularly papers. Thank you so much. Goodbye, Dr. Davie. I'm so glad you could come."

"I have been greatly interested," said Davie. "Thank you both very much."

II

Sitting in the drawing room after lunch, Davie told Miss Eggar what it was that had engaged his attention.

"Am I being ridiculously suspicious? Am I meddling in other people's business? Am I pursuing a possibly dangerous secret?"

Miss Eggar considered. Then, "You are *not* being ridiculously suspicious. You *are* meddling in other people's business. And you *are* pursuing a possibly dangerous secret. As Principal of this college I'm content that you should. I don't at all like the idea that something is being done behind my back—even if it isn't dangerous. I would be very glad if you'd give it your attention. What do you want?"

"I want no publicity. And the key to the new building, and the studio."

"You shall have it."

"Have you a tape recorder?"

"I haven't. Miss Cragg has."

"An official one would be better."

"The music department has one," said Miss Eggar. "I'll borrow it—or if no one's there I'll take it."

"Thank you. So long as you can do it without a fuss. I just wanted to test something."

It was at this moment that Reginald separated himself from the other cats by the fire, and, having made an elaborate pretense of looking out of the window, arrived suddenly on Davie's knee.

"Ooo!" said Davie. Reginald lifted a pink nose and purred ingratiatingly in his face. "All right," said Davie, "you are welcome. But kneading my legs with claws out is forbidden. If you do, that will be the end." Reginald settled down and gazed in a lordly manner at the fire. "I love cats," said Davie, "but I don't own one. One can't in college. Besides I couldn't bear to see my chairs ripped to pieces for one thing, and I couldn't accept the tie for another. I've never been wedded to a person or to an animal. Friendship is better."

"Go on," said Miss Eggar.

"I love to be a host, to entertain, to cherish a friend." Here Reginald turned his head and looked at Davie as though with warm appreciation of this generous design. Davie stroked his back. "With some people," he went on, "I greatly love to be entertained myself. But neither enjoyment implies a state of surrender. The man who marries abandons liberty. He doesn't always enjoy the experience—doesn't often, I believe I could say. I'm sure I wouldn't. It is difficult enough to be free even on your own. It only needs a ring on the telephone or, worse, a ring at the door—and good manners may entrap you."

"Are you sure this isn't an apologia for a selfish bachelor life?"

"Oh no. Selfishness means what it says. But a love of freedom is tempered with a love of other people—in a free condition, in the right proportions, at the right time, in the right place."

"It is difficult to see beyond the barrier," said Miss Eggar, "but in that case dear Reginald is not, as I had sometimes feared, entirely selfish."

"Certainly not. He is comfort-loving but also man-loving," said Davie, stroking Reginald under the chin.

Reginald began to purr again.

"How very satisfactory!" said Miss Eggar. "It is a great relief to be reassured on that point."

"And now," said Davie, "I fear we must put him to the test. I want to go back to the studio to see George Tallent at work. Reginald would prefer me to stay. But on my putting the matter to him reasonably he jumps down. The sagacious animal realizes that the world must go on."

"I shall expect you for tea," said Miss Eggar. "And by then I hope I will have commandeered what you want. Reginald! Leave that chair alone! Just when Dr. Davie has spoken so well of you—"

III

George Tallent turned his head as Davie entered the studio.

"Afternoon, Dr. Davie. Back again?"

"Yes, please. I wanted to see what happens now—though I know it's purely mechanical."

"You're just in time for a gala performance. I'm starting a tape now."

"Tell me what happens."

"Nothing at all that you'd notice. I switch on. You hear the master repeating what you already know by heart—but all the time it's re-re-cording itself on six different machines. They're known as 'slaves' because they obey the master machine in everything. I run the thing through—and six obedient machines produce six copies. It doesn't even have to be watched. I could sit down and read a novel."

"Or talk to me."

"Certainly—but you'll have to put up with the rival conversation." He pressed a button. The spool of recording tape commenced its orderly revolution.

"I wanted to ask you more about this fascinating business," said Davie, raising his voice to compete with Andrew and Daphne's grammatical enthusiasm. "As I understand it, you are dealing with the same people, and if the same people are deliberately working towards one end, you can produce a composite tape which betrays no sign of editing to the ear."

"Right."

"But if someone else played around and altered the tape you would spot the fact because you'd be able to detect a different acoustic, or a different tone, or a mended rhythm."

"Yes."

"I was thinking that one often *is* confused by voices on the wireless. For instance I never have the least idea which is Frank Muir and which is Dennis Norden—and surely one is often deceived on the telephone. If the voice were similar do you think people would necessarily spot a change—especially in a brief extract?"

"I agree you can be deceived if you're not listening for it. I only say that a fiddle would be spotted if it were made the subject of expert examination."

"I see."

"There's another six done," said George Tallent. "They go into their little boxes, join the pile of other little boxes, and Mary collects them in the morning."

"Thank you very much for letting me listen," said Davie. "I mustn't hold you up—and it's time I was off."

As he walked back to the Lodge Davie was thinking that whereas his questions to Mary Cragg had been discreet and natural, his questions to George Tallent had been searching and obvious. If Tallent were engaged in any double dealing Davie would have given himself away completely. But, trusting to instinct and not in the least to common sense or evidence,

Davie did not believe there was a crooked inch in George Tallent's character.

But someone was crooked: he was sure of that. And the tapes were going to stay in the studio till Mary Cragg collected them in the morning. Anybody's game.

IV

After tea Davie retired to his bedroom with the tape recorder filched from the music department. He wanted to listen again to the end of the tape that Miss Eggar had given him. He played it a dozen times, and at the last he thought he could distinguish a different tone. The date of the appointment had not been spoken by Daphne Maiden on some other occasion and afterwards inserted. It had been spoken by a different voice. No doubt a truly dissimilar voice might have stuck out, but for two voices like enough to each other the imposture was nearly perfect. Seven or eight words was so little on which to risk a comparison. Certainly it would never have occurred to Davie to examine the tape if he had not also heard the other one. He had not begun his enquiry because he had noticed any difference. He had begun because he had felt it widely probable that a difference must be there. It did not seem likely that Daphne Maiden had recorded that unexpected rendezvous. But if the alteration had been made without the help of Daphne Maiden, without the skill of George Tallent and without the knowledge of Mary Cragg—who was responsible? It seemed highly improbable now that the question would ever be answered. The interest lay not in the past but in the future. Was anyone going to tamper with the new tape? If so it would have to be done that night after George Tallent's departure. In the morning the tapes were to be collected by Miss Cragg. Something had been said about further copies being made tomorrow. But those might be collected at the end of the day. Tonight was the only sure opportunity.

79

"Yes," said Miss Eggar. "But no one is likely to try till very late. They wouldn't risk being seen. It means a late night, Dr. Davie. It also means that you can have dinner in a civilized manner at a reasonable hour. Is there anything I can do?"

"Yes, please. I can't watch for hours to see if anyone's going in. Could we take it in turns to keep an eye on the place?"

"Certainly—but there's more than one door to the new building. I think we will have to settle ourselves in, on the floor above the studio. There's a sort of reception room there."

"Good," said Davie. "But we'll have to be totally quiet, and we can't have a light, and we might go to sleep."

"We mustn't go to sleep," said Miss Eggar. "I don't see why there shouldn't be a silent service of coffee and cake."

And so, at a quarter past ten, Miss Eggar and Davie left the Lodge, looking as though they had sneaked out from a rather elderly dormitory for the excitements of a midnight feast. Davie was carrying a basket with two cups and a thermos of coffee. Miss Eggar clasped a bag containing Bourbon biscuits and four slices of cherry and almond cake.

"It would be fatuous to walk straight across the lawn," Miss Eggar had said. "Anyone could see us. We must go round behind the rhododendrons, and get in at the side door."

So there they were, walking silently, Davie behind Miss Eggar, screened from the college windows by the evergreens, but on the other side not much protected from the moonlight by the bare limes that fringed the college lands. Once or twice Miss Eggar stopped and listened. A headlamp flashed round the bend in the highroad. An owl sounded its hunting cry over the neighbouring fields. Davie silently commended Miss Eggar's caution. The whole enterprise was possibly absurd. But it would not be worth undertaking at all unless it were taken seriously.

There was a point in the rhododendron walk where an open path turned to the left and led between flower beds to the side entrance of the new building. Miss Eggar paused and listened. Then, after glancing at Davie to make sure he was ready for the final advance, she led the way to the door, avoiding the path and walking on the grass.

"Now," said Miss Eggar, when she had locked the door behind them. "We go up these back stairs and along the corridor. Our room is just the other side of the main staircase. It's also over the studio. We shan't hear anything. But you can make sorties down the stairs. Come on."

The corridor was dark, but it was straight: from the beginning they could see the landing ahead of them, lit by the moon shining through the high staircase window.

They crossed the landing and entered the dark corridor beyond. Then, outside the first door on the right Miss Eggar stopped, listened, and turned the handle. They entered a small reception room. It was well lighted by the night sky. "Here we are," said Miss Eggar softly. "The studio is immediately below. You go and do your stuff. I'll wait here for you."

Davie retraced his steps to the gallery at the top of the main stairs. From the hall below came the steady tick of a grandfather clock.

The new building was a very splendid piece of work. It had been made possible by the equal pride and generosity of Lord Binns, a local magnate who had made an inordinate amount of money by doing something new and not quite fair to the potato. Binns Potato Crumples had swept the market. And here were the fruits. The new laboratories were large and well equipped and the general appointments were lavish.

Davie was looking over an oak gallery from which a double stair curved down to the hall. Opposite, on either side of the grandfather clock were paintings by Constable. On the other two sides of the great space hung big modern pictures—lovely vague fantasies of grass and poppies in nobby chunks of paint. In the center of the hall a bowl of daffodils and willows stood on the shining surface of a fine walnut table.

And on the shining surface of the oak floor lay the shadow of a man.

Davie drew back hastily. Presently he peeped over the gallery again. The shadow was still there. Its owner, out of sight beneath the gallery, must be standing incautiously by the long moonlit window. Davie could feel his heart beating in his neck. Did any shadow ever lie so still? It would wear him out, he felt sure. He would be bound to move first. And then he realized that that would be precisely true. The figure standing in the moonlight beneath the gallery was the stone effigy of Lord Binns. Davie subsided on a small settee out of sight from the hall. Frighted by false fire? Yes, indeed. He was sweating all over. He was, he supposed, too old for these adventures.

For some minutes he sat there listening to the ticking of the clock. Perhaps he closed his eyes. Perhaps he fell into a light doze for a few minutes. It could not have been for long. The clock in the hall was only pointing to ten minutes to twelve when he started up and peered over the gallery again. He had (he thought) felt a light breath of colder air. He had (he felt sure) heard a distant click. At first he thought it was the grandfather clock making up its mind to strike, but ten minutes to the hour was too early for that. Then, as he stood there listening, he heard a faint noise from the corridor beyond the hall. No key is quite silent, no handle turns without a sound, no latch returns to its place without a snip; or if they do sometimes achieve this perfection they do not do so all together at the same time. Davie had heard no steps, but he knew for certain that someone had entered the recording room.

A minute later he was speaking softly to Miss Eggar. "Someone's there. In the studio. Will you watch from the landing? I'm going down."

Miss Eggar nodded.

"Come on," said Davie.

On the moonlit gallery they stood listening. They heard only the tick of the great clock. Davie lifted a finger. Again Miss Eggar nodded. Then very carefully he stepped down the stairs.

From the hall he turned into the corridor, and halted. Faintly from the recording room came a sound that held him motionless. Someone was playing *Tosca*.

There was no square of light in the studio door. Presumably that meant that the visitor was working by torchlight. Davie tip-toed down the corridor. He hoped he could see something through the little window. He was disappointed. He could see nothing at all. Then gradually he became aware of a faint line of light on the left edge of the glass. He was not going to see anything. The window had a curtain and it had been drawn.

He waited. Tick-tock. Tick-tock. Tick-tock. There was no other sound. And then, suddenly, on the other side of the door, a voice said "We can do that on the way home": and a girl's voice added, "On Wednesday the twenty-ninth." Daphne's voice. Or was it Daphne's voice? As on the other tape, four words had been added. It seemed to be the same voice, but how could one judge on so little? Silence returned. Tick-tock, tick-tock, tick-tock. Presently the same words were repeated, "We can do that on the way home." "On Wednesday the twenty-ninth." And this time the music from *Tosca* followed to give the thing an ending. Then after another silence the whole tape began at the beginning.

Even Davie could understand what was happening. The original tape had been given two additions, and it was now being copied by the "slave" recording machines. When it was finished there would be six copies of the altered tape. If that was what he wanted, all the visitor would have to do would be to remove the two additions from the original tape, and no one would know that it had ever been touched.

Davie took his diary from his pocket. As best he could in the darkness he wrote down "Wednesday the twenty-ninth." Then he went back to the gallery.

The person in the studio could hardly be finished for ten minutes. It would be easy to wait outside the door—but that would wreck the larger opportunity. Once it was known the matter was being investigated the investigation became worthless. The needful thing was to spot the person without being spotted.

"We must go outside," said Miss Eggar.

"How many doors are there?"

"Three. The main door—"

"He won't use that."

"And the two side doors—the one we used and the one at the opposite end of the building."

"Come on," said Davie. "You watch the door we came in at. I'll watch the other one. It's nearer the studio. I think he'll use that one."

Silently they made their way along the corridor and back down the stairs. Miss Eggar unlocked the door and locked it again behind them.

"That's your path," she said. "Follow the building. You'll recognize the door."

The moon had lost itself behind a bank of clouds. A mist had risen from the river. The rhododendron hedge ten yards away was almost invisible.

"He won't be easy to see," said Davie.

"I don't know why you keep saying 'he'," said Miss Eggar. "This is a women's college."

VI

The mist had grown thicker and Davie was very cold. He had been waiting for fifteen minutes behind a rhododendron bush and he had heard nothing except, once, the sound of a car at the bend in the road beneath the trees, and, once, the call of that insatiable owl. He had almost decided that the visitor must have chosen the other exit, when, suddenly, across the gravel path that lay between him and the building came the faint sound of a turning key. In the darkness he felt rather than saw that the door had opened and that a figure had quickly turned its back on him to lock it again.

It had not occurred to Davie that the person in the studio would attempt any measure of concealment. Peering through the rhododendron bush not five yards from the door, he felt sure he would see something. But the figure that disappeared into the darkness three seconds later was dressed in black and wore a scarf covering its face—whether by design or as a protection against the mist was no matter. Davie saw nothing at all except a pair of trousers. In this part of the exercise he had failed completely. The only satisfactory aspect of the failure was that he had not betrayed himself. The person in the studio did not know that he had been overheard.

There was no point in waiting a moment longer. Feeling rather foolish, Davie made his way back to the other door.

"We don't seem to have been very successful," Miss Eggar said later over a glass of whisky and hot milk.

"I don't know about that," said Davie. "We have collected a second example of this peculiar mystery. And it *is* a mystery. No one would go to all that trouble just for fun. The person who has provided us with the clue may not be of particular importance in the problem."

But in his heart he was cross with himself. If trousers meant anything it was a man. But as Miss Eggar had remarked, "This is a women's college." The modern girl wore trousers. The modern woman wore trousers. Miss Cragg herself wore trousers.

At which point a curious thought came into his head. It led to his saying a minute or so later, "I don't think just anyone could have done that work. They must have had some experience in editing."

"Yes," said Miss Eggar. "Certainly they must. Have some more whisky."

"Thanks. In the morning I'd like to have a look at the studio."

"Mr. Tallent won't be there before nine-thirty."

"I'd like to go in at half past eight."

"I will accompany you," said Miss Eggar. "That totally unnecessary picnic must be retrieved."

6

I

Davie was in the train, dividing his attention between the scenery and the advertisement cards. They were spinning past a chain of large back gardens, nine in ten of them competitively stocked with roses. What would the effect be in June? Davie was beginning to have doubts about roses. Nowadays there were so many of them—roses in hedges, roses in beds, roses climbing up walls, roses showering down pergolas. He hardly liked to confess so traitorous a thought, but roses—it seemed to him—had become the Englishman's vice. The trouble was that these days they were backed by little wooden sheds and glass houses, and yellow bricks and bedroom windows. "A rose is a rose is a rose" (that we may take as established, he thought, and wasn't it odd that that was the only line of Gertrude Stein's that anyone remembered?) but a rose is much more a rose among green lawns or against a yew hedge. The modern suburban gardener did not seem to know this. Davie thought they should give the roses a rest. What the small garden wanted was a proliferation of herbaceous bordery.

Beyond the houses it was sometimes possible to see a fringe of the woods that still bore the title of a forest. It was an antidote to all those roses.

Davie turned his attention to the car cards. Immediately opposite to him was one of those frank appeals to mankind to sweeten themselves. This campaign against a human frailty had been waged for at least fifty years and apparently in vain. All the deodorants were in as great supply as ever—and all with such tricksy names. The one in front of him was called No-O-Dor, which cleverly imparted a Persian flavour to the promised relief. Davie exercised his mind on a suitable name for an alternate product. He had to admit that it was difficult. No-O-Dor was much more likely to attract the sufferer than his own more robust Smelavaunt. Avaunt was too recondite a word—but sixty years ago he remembered advertisements which presumed a public with some judgment in words. There had been Antipon, for instance, which in the days of his youth had figured so largely in the weekly magazines. What would the modern housewife make of Antipon? It would have to be called Eezyslim before she recognized the splendid opportunity that lay within her swallow.

However occupied the mind, nobody thinks of one thing exclusively. In the middle of a desperate decision the fly on the window obtrudes itself. Davie was really thinking about the adventures of the previous night, but they were woven imperceptibly with suburban roses, and the crying need for deodorants. There was also a man with a soup-strainer moustache, such as he had not beheld for many years.

He had been in the studio early—but there was nothing of interest to his untrained eyes. The place was tidy. There was a short piece of tape in the basket and he had annexed it. It might be the addition that last night's visitor had made to George Tallent's tape. But even if it were it would not tell him anything.

The situation was peculiar. It was not for him to go to the police. Miss Eggar could go to them on the ground that an unauthorized person had committed a trespass in the college buildings. But she was against this. She did not want an excitement in the college. Besides, what would the police find? Fingerprints? Possibly—but almost certainly not known ones. It would be far better, they both agreed, if Davie could find out a bit more by his own private researches.

He had looked in his engagement book. Late that month there was indeed such a day as Wednesday the twenty-ninth. But the key to the puzzle was the music. *Tosca*? On that date *Tosca* was not being performed in London, or anywhere else in Britain. That Davie knew for certain. If the recording really did make an appointment, then there was something in it that he had not understood.

He looked out of the window. They were nearing London now. The large back gardens and the houses fringed by the forest had given way to dark and very small backyards, and these grew laundry lines instead of roses.

And then the train plunged downwards into the earth and that was the end of the sunlit world. The windows became mysterious looking glasses, maliciously doubling foreheads, eyes, and noses. Davie thought his double nose was particularly entertaining. He adjusted his doubled bow tie.

There were really two problems. What did the message mean? And who was responsible for sending it? The first might perhaps be determined by thought. The second meant asking questions. But he had no authority to ask questions. And if he asked questions of the right persons he would betray his interest: and if he asked questions of the wrong ones their answers would not be worth collecting. There were several people he would like to question. George Tallent, Daphne Maiden (who was probably as simple as she looked), Mary Cragg, Andrew Wynne, and, yes, Dr. Marie Baendels.

But it was Andrew he wanted to talk to first. He had a feeling he could speak plainly to Andrew.

And then it was Holborn, and five minutes later Davie was leaving his case with old Frank at the Gainsborough.

"I've been on safari in furthest Essex, Frank," he said.

"You'll be a lot safer here with us, Dr. Davie," said Frank.

Safer? The word added something to Davie's speculations. But he was not quite sure what.

"Yes," said the aged Frank again, apparently under the impression that he had said something extremely entertaining, "you'll be a lot safer here with us, Dr. Davie."

II

He did not stay long at the Gainsborough. The unexpected visit to London had given him the chance to arrange lunch in Putney with an old friend of his mother, Dame Alice Grainger. This remarkable old party of ninety-two lived in a Victorian house, richly furnished in the Edwardian taste, and was waited on by a handmaid called Florence, who wore that original magenta-striped dress dedicated to late Victorian housemaids, with white cuffs and apron, and a cap with vestigial bands. Florence was sixty-five and she knew exactly the stately tradition of her calling.

Davie always went to see Dame Alice whenever he could. She talked with engaging familiarity about Algernon Swinburne and Watts-Dunton, as though they still lived just round the corner, and Oscar Wilde, and Lily Langtry, and Mrs. Pankhurst, and often, when he left her house he would return to his old grief about the size of the historian's mesh, which let so much of interest slip away for ever. One day Dame Alice told him about the death, at Clifton, of Thomas Adolphus Trollope, whom she had known as a girl. "His grave was covered with a beautiful mosaic, brought from Italy," she said. "Do you know, within a few months, the whole thing was dug up and stolen." Perhaps somewhere in the old thieves' area of Bristol, Davie would muse, there is some dingy backyard paved with the coloured stones that were brought so far to honour the historian of Florence. And then he would think of the robbers of the tombs of the Pharaohs and wonder whether their spoil was yet remaining in the world. Some of it surely must be. You can lose precious stones. You don't destroy them.

The impending visit to Dame Alice had brought this memory to mind as he sat now on top of a No. 14 bus, just halted at Piccadilly Circus. He was sorry the flower sellers had been moved from the fountain steps. The old girls had looked deliciously unlikely targets for Eros, but they had added colour to the place and (like hansom cabs) they had belonged to the statue's beginning. They had been "period". The young people who now lolled on the steps were also "period". But they did not add colour.

The bus slewed round the corner and turned into the Haymarket.

Between Piccadilly and Knightsbridge the bus seemed to be more often standing still than moving, and "I there before thee," murmured Davie to himself as, like Robert Bridges, he kept reaching the end of his journey before the bus had hardly started on it. But they got along better as soon as they had found the Fulham Road, and there he was pleased to see the old Town Hall, where he and Frederick Dyke had often suffered at the resurrection of some early and forgotten work. Posters were out for Puccini's *Edgar* at the beginning of April, and of course he would be going. Puccini, yes: but not on Wednesday the twenty-ninth.

The bus moved on, and Davie fell into a light doze, which held him in its beneficent embraces until the end of his journey. And after a short walk he reached Dame Alice's house almost exactly at the appointed time.

III

Lunching with Dame Alice was always a gastronomic experience because Emma, the cook, who had been with Dame Alice almost as long as Florence, was in the way of serving, in the most natural manner, the kind of dishes which people can no longer be bothered to cook at home, and which restaurants consider out of their line.

"Boiled leg of lamb with dumplings!" said Davie. "We always had it when I was young. One never meets it now. I haven't seen a dumpling for years. And caper sauce. What bliss! Dame Alice, you are a great hostess."

"Thank you, R.V.—but pray tell me what a great hostess is."

"That's easy," said Davie. "The art of being a hostess consists in giving guests what they like—whether it's food, bed-clothes, conversation, or croquet—without allowing them to suspect that any trouble has gone to the achievement. The well-run house apparently runs on its own. Great hostesses know what's needed by magic."

"Florence, please give Dr. Davie some more lamb," said Dame Alice. "And a dumpling."

"You see!" said Davie.

After the lamb there were French pancakes, the kind you bake in the oven—something never seen in a restaurant and something the modern housewife has never heard of. Davie knew them of old. "Well done, Emma," he said. Which was duly reported to the kitchen by Florence.

After luncheon they sat in the famous drawing-room, which included in its furnishings the manners of the best part of a century. There was the William Morris paper at one end of the story and a Joan Eardley painting at the other and in between the portrait bust by Epstein and the Beerbohm cartoons. The once fashionable silver framed photographs had all been swept away. "My dear R.V.," said Dame Alice, "I have a whole cupboard full of silver frames and boxes and ornamental pairs of scissors. They must be worth a fortune. When I die it will be like unlocking a funerary chamber in one of the pyramids. And they incommoded the lid of the piano. I still play, you know, just for my own pleasure between ten and eleven every morning. What do you think of pop music, R.V.? I've listened to it on the wireless."

"It's quite entertaining sometimes—but it's all the same."

Dame Alice nodded her head.

"Ah—yes. That is so. And it's a curious thing that the words should always be so flagrantly untrue."

"Music has a power to suspend disbelief."

"Certainly," said Dame Alice. "'I'm for ever blowing bubbles,' for instance. And can you imagine anything more boring than being on a slow boat to China with anyone, let alone the object of your alleged affections?"

Davie marvelled at the extent of Dame Alice's listening.

"When I was a young woman," she went on, "there was a very popular song extolling the virtues of an old-fashioned house—"

"I remember."

"It contained the remarkable admission that the singer loved every mouse in that old-fashioned house—a statement which seems to me far less probable than the entire story of *Aida*, and yet momentarily made to appear sincere by the alchemy of music." Dame Alice drained her coffee cup. "Of course," she added, "if the mouse had not been made out to be such a tricksy sweet little thing by Miss Beatrix Potter even music could not have held the words together."

"Dame Alice," said Davie. "I want to ask your advice."

"Yes, R.V.?"

Davie told her his problem.

"Now, tell me, Dame Alice—if the music of *Rigoletto* makes a direct reference to a performance of *Rigoletto* at Covent Garden on a certain date, why doesn't the music of *Tosca* make a direct reference to a performance of *Tosca*?"

"Isn't one. You said so."

"Then what does it refer to?"

"Music by Puccini."

"But there isn't any Puccini on that date."

"Then there must be an amateur performance somewhere."

"I would think that happily improbable."

"Then," said Dame Alice, "there is a society that puts on opera. Something with a name like Musica Resurrecta, I would think."

"There are several societies that put on opera. They are not performing that night."

"Then there is another society you don't know about."

"Thank you," said Davie. "You grind me down to a point. Somewhere there is Puccini."

"Of course," said Dame Alice. Then she added, "There must be a code book—something the recipients can refer to. Something in the form of a calendar."

"You're right—and it couldn't be a calendar dealing with hole-in-corner stuff. A calendar that referred to *Rigoletto* and Covent Garden on one occasion would have to be the same calendar that referred to *Tosca* on another."

"There are the advertisement lists in the big papers—but that costs money. I don't think the obscure production would be recorded there, as a reliable rule."

"And there's *Opera*," said Davie—"comes out every month and records everything."

"Surely you take it?"

"Yes—and so does the Chesterfield. But I don't remember seeing any other Puccini, and I read it pretty carefully."

"You get a copy, R.V.," said Dame Alice. "Get it quickly. And now—"

"I know," said Davie. "It's time for your rest. Time for mine too if I can get back soon enough. Thank you so much for a lovely lunch, and for your help."

Dr. Davie lifted Dame Alice's hand and kissed it. He was not in the habit of kissing ladies' hands, but Dame Alice was someone very special.

IV

Davie would have missed it even if he had been awake on the last part of his bus ride to Putney, for St. Botolph's Assembly Hall was on the other side of the road and at half past twelve it would have displayed nothing of interest for him. But on his way back to London he was wide awake and the bus stopped exactly beside that unlovely edifice. The bus had evidently been going too fast and the conductor for prudential reasons was holding up for a minute at this stop. Somewhere around the corner an Inspector lurked with a watch.

There was a board outside on which an elderly man, who seemed to have conceived a profound disgust for his life's calling, was desperately engaged in sticking a notice. The top bit was secure, the rest under the influence of a malign March wind was curling itself about in a manner which seemed to threaten the ancient manipulator with the fate of Laocoon.

Davie marvelled at the old man's inefficiency. Twice he unstuck the bill. The second time he tore it and had to produce another from his bag. All this suffering for what? Davie wondered. A bazaar? A jumble sale? A lantern lecture on the work of the church in North Borneo? A concert by the Youth Club?

The conductor rang his bell. Looking over his shoulder as they started, Davie saw the old man fasten the fluttering poster on the board with a vicious slap of his brush. And at the same moment a jovial wind caught up the discarded poster and smacked it against Davie's window. The Pro-Opera Society, he read—eh? What was that? The Pro-Opera Society would present—here the poster was crumpled—it was not clear what they would present—but the name Puccini was clear and so was the date: March 28 and 29. Then high in the air the poster whirled as though enjoying its impropriety and stuck itself inelegantly in the branches of a cherry tree.

Davie rang the bell and got off at the request stop. By the time he had made his way back the ancient bill-sticker had retired, doubtless to consume a cup of restorative tea in some subterranean cavern provided by the charity of St. Botolph.

The poster was even now slightly askew and rumpled, but Davie learned that the Pro-Opera Society proposed to present *Manon Lescaut* as its first production on March 28 and 29. The seats would be 15/-, 10/-, and 5/-. Old Age Pensioners half price. "Old Age Pensioner be damned," thought Davie, "why will they fling it in one's face?" He resolved to buy two 15/- seats at full price and to invite Chief Inspector Mays to accompany him.

Three minutes later he was on top of a bus again. *Manon Lescaut*: March 29: it seemed to him to make sense. Not everyone is an operatic expert, but almost anyone knows the really famous arias. If, on the night you want to fix a meeting, you cannot draw attention to an exact opera, you can at least draw attention to an exact composer. Look in the code book—and probably it's *Opera*—you'll find there's only one Puccini on that night—and most conveniently it's at an obscure assembly hall in West London. It made sense all right: but why? Why these tortuous devices? Who was going to meet whom? And for what purpose?

V

Davie got off the 14 bus at the request stop before Green Park and made his way through Shepherd Market to the Chesterfield.

It was the dead part of the afternoon. Craddock was half-asleep, and the club looked deserted. Davie walked down the corridor past the dining room, and turned left towards the four telephone boxes which stood opposite the cloakroom. In the first he caught the side view of Willy

Marchant giving a complete performance to an unseen auditor at the other end of the line. Davie moved on to the fourth box and consulted directory S—Z. The name was there. It was probably right. He dialled. The number was engaged. That was encouraging. At least there was someone in.

Davie tried again and was rewarded by a series of angry pips. He always found those pips very agitating: they seemed to suggest there was not a second to lose. Besides he found it extremely difficult to push the money in.

"Yes?" said a rather sleepy voice.

"Can I speak to Andrew Wynne?"

"Andrew Wynne here."

"Ah—this is R. V. Davie speaking. I met you yesterday—"

"Yes, indeed—" the voice sounded suddenly awake.

"I wanted to ask if we might meet," said Davie. "I'm interested in that recording work, and I wanted to ask some questions from someone who really knows about it."

"I don't know that I know very much," said Andrew Wynne after a perceptible pause.

"I know nothing at all," said Davie, "and I shall be grateful for your help."

"What do you suggest?"

"Well let me see," said Davie. "I'm at the Chesterfield Club at the moment. Why not drop in for a drink . . . Hallo? Are you there?"

There had been so sudden a silence at the other end that it almost sounded as though the line were dead.

"Yes, I'm here," said Andrew.

"I thought we'd been cut off. Well—could you do that?"

"Er—no, Dr. Davie, I don't think I could very well. I—"

"Look here," said Davie, "I've a better idea. May *I* drop in and see *you*?"

"Not today," said Andrew. "I'm sorry but I'm fixed."

"Well, tomorrow then. Sunday morning. I could call about noon if that suited you."

"If you don't mind doing that, Dr. Davie, I'll be delighted." Suddenly he seemed to have recovered his spirits.

"Thank you very much. I'll be with you at twelve. Good-bye."

He was pleased that it had fallen out that way. It would be much better to see Andrew in his own surroundings.

As Davie left the telephone box the club secretary came out of the cloakroom.

"Hullo, Davie," he said. "Any news?"

"None at all."

"No sign of Robbin?"

"Not that I know."

In the hall Willy Marchant was talking to Craddock. Some communication vitally important to the educational system of Britain had gone astray.

Frederick Dyke was mounting the stairs. Looking over his shoulder, he said, "You're very lively. You're usually asleep at this time of day," and proceeded on his way without looking for an answer. Davie waved a hand at him and entered the writing room.

Not a great deal of writing went on in the writing room. It was the quiet room, the room where the magazines were. Davie hunted through them all. Not finding what he wanted, he chose an evening paper, rang a bell, and sank gratefully into a deep armchair. When the waiter came he ordered tea.

Meantime, the paper. On page one there was a very newsworthy disaster in Venezuela. On page two our special correspondent from Salisbury, Rhodesia, had something to report. On pages three and four he studied the picture of Linda Titmuss, who was taking a leading part in an amateur performance of *Rose Marie*, of Amy Snapper who had just jumped an incredible distance up in the air, and of Madge Masters who had been elected Carnival Queen of somewhere. He decided he liked Amy Snapper best. Madge looked conceited. It was unlikely that Linda could sing. But Amy, though never destined to win a Beauty Competition, could plainly jump. He liked the dedicated competence to do something well. "Three cheers for Amy Snapper," said Davie just loud enough to cause Adrian Ballsover to look at him over the top of *The Economist* from a neighbouring armchair.

Adrian Ballsover was a person who was interviewed by the B.B.C. on subjects like the gap in the sterling balances. And he was able to use words like "accreditation" and "in-span" in his ordinary conversation— which always astonished Davie very much. Davie shrank into his jacket and pretended to be deeply absorbed in an article about the failure of an insurance company. Then, after skipping the Prime Minister's observations on wages and prices, and reading every word of the gossip page, he came eventually to an article about the drug traffic, just as the waiter arrived with his tea. At the moment tea was the drug which concerned him. He laid the paper down. But it was a well contrived article, and, two pieces of toast and three cups of tea later, he returned to it.

The problem was distribution. Those that had the poison had to be extremely ingenious. Once a man was marked as a drug man he was useless. There had to be constant changes among the people who worked the racket, and in the way they worked it. A church had recently been used. The vicar had found drugs that had been left there either by design or accident.

"Our church is open to all," the vicar had told our special correspondent. "Our doors are never closed. How can we guarantee that those who enter God's house have come for the right reason? Two people kneel near each other in a pew. Have they come to pray? Or will one of them leave a small parcel on the seat which the other will appropriate?"

The author of the article went on to explain how quickly the scene must change to suit the safety of the racketeer. It would never work if any particular place was a recognized rendezvous. Trafalgar Square was all right, perhaps, for the small-timer. But the real organizers needed something safer than that: they had to think fast and move fast. Just for once Madame Tussaud's might make a meeting place, or the British Museum, or the Wallace Collection, but nowhere was safe for long. The big men at the top had to organize their trade as skilfully as a foreign embassy organizes its network of spies.

"Do not look for the big shots in Trafalgar Square," wrote the journalist. "Do not, indeed, look for them anywhere. They are careful to keep in the background. But do not look for the agents of the big shots in Trafalgar Square either. They are much more likely to have arranged a meeting at an exhibition of modern paintings or a spring collection of new daffodils. Given some code the same people could meet each other in the most unlikely places with guaranteed safety. Safe distribution depends on an ingenious system."

Davie read the last two sentences again. It was impossible not to be reminded of the Language Course tapes. A code. An appointment. Surely they were precisely that. There had been an altered tape in December which seemed to make an appointment at Covent Garden on January 4. And here in March was another altered tape which seemed to make an appointment for March 29 at, or possibly at, a West London hall. Someone was going to great trouble to make these tapes. There must be a bad reason.

But was such a plan over-elaborate? Davie did not think so. Telephone calls can be tapped. Letters can be opened. Callers can be watched. But this hidden instruction, if that was what it was, was intelligible only to the person expecting it—and the meeting arranged would not even be clandestine. It was to take place under the noses of several hundred people. It was a very ingenious plan. Davie could feel his imagination racing ahead of him. There was no evidence at all that this curious prank at St. Martha's was in aid of the drug trade. But it might be. Certainly it was in aid something.

He returned to the newspaper, and "These people will stop at nothing," he read. "If murder is necessary to protect their trade, then they will do murder."

Murder. It was no good. Everything compelled his thoughts in one direction. Murder could suggest to his mind nobody but Brent—and Brent had heard that tape only an hour or so before he was killed. He had heard the important part of it three times. And he was a policeman. If the wrong person had overheard him wouldn't he have thought that Brent was investigating the matter? And if they'd thought that mightn't they have "stopped at nothing"? It would have been perfectly easy to overhear . . . and then Davie suddenly smacked his knee and got another glance from Adrian Ballsover. Somebody had certainly been there—the person who had gone into the bathroom and left the door bolted. It might have been a housemaid, or it might not have been a housemaid. Thought by thought he was building up a fantastic idea. Someone at the Chesterfield with an interest in the drug traffic? It was grotesque. "People don't do such things", as Judge Brack would have said if he had been a member of the club. But people did so such things.

Davie was not pleasantly excited by his thought. He had enjoyed considering the problem of St. Martha's Language Course, but he had never expected it to lead him back to Brent. He was sensitive about his reputation as an amateur prodnose, and he didn't want to go to the police with a far-fetched theory about the murder case. They'd only think him an interfering fool. The whole thing was speculation. And yet the more he thought about it the more certain he was that he would have to speak.

He decided to go back to the Gainsborough and to telephone Mays from there.

Davie walked across the hall to the morning room, which was empty, and looked at the magazines there. Then he went for his hat and coat. As he passed through the hall on his way out he said to Alfred, who had relieved Craddock, "What's happened to this month's *Opera*, Alfred? It's not in the morning room or the writing room."

"*Opera*?" said Alfred. "We don't take *Opera*, Dr. Davie."

"Of course we do, Alfred. I've seen it here."

"Someone might have left a copy lying about some time, sir, but we don't take it. I've got a list."

"How very odd!" said Davie, wrinkling his forehead. "I must be going barmy. But you must know, Alfred. Sorry to have bothered you. Good night"

It was five o'clock.

VI

It was five o'clock. In his flat on the ground floor of a house in Elm Park Road, Chelsea, Andrew Wynne, comfortably reclining in an armchair, set down his teacup and referred again to a piece of paper. It was a carbon copy of a short list of addresses, and the names afforded him considerable amusement. The Reverend Samuel Corke of St. Wilfred's Vicarage, Potter Street, Birmingham: Mr. Miffin of Leeds: Mr. Tuffy of Glasgow: the Reverend James Mugg of Liverpool: the Reverend Arthur Grumble (particularly good, that one) of Manchester: and Miss Ellen Masterbridge of Newcastle. What, he wondered were they all up to, this stuffy set of collaborators?

He was still feeling a bit boss-eyed. He had not got to bed till after three o'clock and had slept until one. Then he had taken his time. He had only climbed out of his bath when Jacko called at two o'clock, and he had let him in, clothed more in steam than anything else. It was fortunate. Jacko had had to get the lunch, which was precisely what Andrew had been dreading doing. The whisky and ginger ale had been comforting. The scrambled egg had been eaten Roman fashion, lying on a Regency sofa, draped (up to a point, said Jacko) in a bath towel.

After Jacko had gone and Andrew had at last managed to dress himself, that strange old gentleman, Dr. Davie, had rung up from the Chesterfield Club, and was not to be put off by Andrew not having the smallest intention of going near the place. And now it was five o'clock and he had only just finished writing home and doing up parcels. He hated parcels. Just as some gardeners had green fingers so some people seemed to have brown fingers, they were so deft with paper and string. Not Andrew—he hated it.

He poured himself out another cup of tea. In five minutes he really must get to the mail box. He wondered what old Davie really wanted. Was it only ordinary questions about recording? If it were nothing deeper than that he could manage, but certainly it would never have done to meet him at the Chesterfield.

Andrew heaved himself out of his chair, and took a peek at himself in the long looking glass. He ran a comb through his fair wavy hair. It was long but not too long. In grey trousers with a white stripe and a high-necked navy blue sweater he thought he looked rather nice. Then he let himself out of the door, turned right and right again into The Vale. He had decided to go to the big post office opposite the Town Hall. He wanted the walk.

The Reverend Samuel Corke, Mr. Miffin, Mr. Tuffy, the Reverend James Mugg, the Reverend Arthur Grumble, and Miss Ellen Masterbridge: he took them with him. How were these honest citizens involved in this vague adventure? Andrew turned it over in his mind, but it was difficult to concentrate on the problem in the King's Road with all those amusing people to look at and all those shop windows to see himself in, and all those antique shops to enjoy, and all the kinky clothes shops. He was feeling refreshed already. It was good to be out among all these evidences of a living world—much better than sitting at home, wondering if the telephone were going to ring, and, if it did ring, whether it was going to be his agent with a lovely job, or somebody he'd seen more than enough of.

He posted his parcels.

Then, already lighter in heart, he went back to the flat, added to his attire a pair of tall boots and a leather jacket, and went off to meet Jacko at a restaurant in the Earls Court Road.

`VII

It was about nine o'clock when they turned in at the Flying Horse. The place was jammed to the door, the atmosphere hot and thick with smoke. At one end of the big saloon someone was playing a piano. No one could hear a note at six yards distance. Here and there a few adventurous women had installed themselves at the small tables. No one except their escorts took the smallest notice of them. It was a man's pub, mostly a young man's pub, a jeans and leather jacket affair. A few of the more flamboyant were indulging the new passions for uniforms. A diminutive young man in a guardsman's scarlet tunic was plainly absurd. But the fair one in a jacket that had once belonged to a naval officer was really rather splendid: and knew it.

Andrew looked around him. He never could think why he came. He knew several people there, but he was bored by their facetious conversation. He didn't like beer. And he didn't like the masquerade that it all was, everyone really acting a part and dressed for it. And yet he came there and dressed for it himself. He would have been happier at a concert; happier far if anyone had seen fit to occupy his evenings by giving him a part in a play. But things did not go that way with him. He was better known as the young man on the telly who kept advising the British housewife what to waste her money on next. He did it well but it did not occupy his evenings, and so he came to the Flying Horse and drank things he didn't like, played a part that he didn't really believe in, and sometimes did things he didn't enjoy. That was the curious part about it.

He looked round for Jacko. Jacko had drifted into a corner with four or five friends. He got on much better in this company than Andrew did.

Andrew felt suddenly angry with himself. He was tired and he wanted to go home. Why be so fatuously weak? He pushed his way over to Jacko.

"I'm off."

"Off! It's only half past nine."

"I know, but I've had it for today."

"O.K."

Jacko waved an amiable hand. He was easy with everyone.

Andrew shouldered his way through the scrum. Outside the door he drew a deep breath. It was cold, March cold, and lovely after that fetid atmosphere. He turned right and set off towards the Boltons.

"Going my way?" said the man who had followed him out of the pub.

7

I

"Thank you. Dr. Davie," Mays had said when Davie had finished his story. "It seems to me there are two problems: the murder of Morris Brent, and this queer story about the recording tapes. They may have nothing to do with each other."

Davie nodded.

"But suppose for a moment that they could be connected—then I see two difficulties. The first is an obvious one. It does seem improbable that a member of the Chesterfield Club would be in such a racket."

"Certainly it does. That would be the best possible shield."

"It would. But criminals can't just say 'We'll operate in such and such a place because it's unlikely.' Lambeth Palace would be a splendid head-quarters—if you could get in."

"The other objection?"

"It seems improbable in the circumstances that the tape would go forward. If no one heard it that day then the possible connection between the death and the tape collapses. If someone did hear it—wouldn't they cancel the whole operation rather than risk being caught?"

"That is a point, I agree: but there are two answers. First, it was an old tape, not the current one—which indeed hadn't even been made then: and, second, there would be no risk at all if you nobbled your man quickly. Brent was dead within two and a half hours of hearing the tape." Davie wrinkled his forehead. "And it was I who got him to play it."

"Dr. Davie—if your theory is true, doesn't it occur to you that you equally would be in danger of your life?"

"Yes, I have thought of that, and observed with gratitude that after five days I am still here. From that I deduce—supposing my suggestion to be true—that the listener did not know that anyone else was in the room. Suppose he was passing the door and heard the tape as it began. Suppose he went into the bathroom and listened until Brent had played that end part three times over—mightn't he have felt that he'd heard enough, that he had better not betray himself, that he had better get away somewhere to think things out—without ever hearing my voice at all?"

"It is possible."

"Find a better reason! The man was killed upon the property of the Chesterfield Club. It must have been done by someone who was in the habit of using the place."

"Not 'must'," said Mays. For several seconds he did not speak. He was, Davie noticed, drawing a picture of a man with a big nose. Very carefully he added large shaggy eyebrows. Then he added a moustache. Then he gave him an eye-glass. Then he said, "Look here, Dr. Davie, I don't know that I'm convinced by the part of your theory which connects the tape with Brent's murder. But I am impressed by your story of the altered tapes. I agree that that could be concerned with something very important indeed. It would be dreadfully silly to take so much trouble over some sort of a joke."

"Exactly."

"Well, then, I shall be very grateful for your help. Go to see this young man. You could get something out of him."

Davie got up and said goodbye. At the door he paused, his hand on the handle. "That theory of mine could be absolutely wrong—and yet the tapes and the murder could be connected in some other way."

Mays stared at him.

"Sorry—that was a totally unhelpful remark," said Davie. "Goodnight."

And so here he was on the top of a No. 22 bus, heading for Chelsea at half past eleven on a March Sunday.

There had been rain during the night. Now everything glistened in the sun. The budding daffodils at Hyde Park Corner were a sheet of green and gold. Poor old Wordsworth would have had a seizure if he could have seen them, thought Davie. And later, as the bus traversed Sloane Street he was misquoting Housman to himself:

> Now of my three-score years and ten
> Seventy will not come again.

Really, it did not bear joking about. There were no cherries hung with snow yet, but he screwed his head round to get what could always be a last look at an almond tree.

Fortunately for him Davie had a mind like a kaleidoscope. When he turned into Sloane Square and saw the advertisement for *The Three*

Sisters he was briefly lost in memory of the production he had seen in the thirties when every member of the cast either was already, or would be, famous. And then the Court Theatre dissolved into Covent Garden, and just as easily did Covent Garden dissolve into the front cover of *Opera.* Davie suddenly controlled his mind and kept *Opera* fixed in the middle of his forehead. *Opera.* He was thinking about it because he had not been able to find it at the Chesterfield and yet he was certain he had seen it there within the last few days. He could positively see it lying on a table with a lot of other magazines. It was rather a splendid table, and "I must be going potty," Davie said to himself, "because we haven't got a table like that in—" and there he stopped. It was Beaufort Street and he had to get out. Opposite the stop was the smallest bookshop in the world. In the window were Indian pictures painted on mica. Davie forgot about *Opera.* These were the pictures all those Indian Civil Service great-uncles used to bring home—provided they had not died of malaria before they could get there. Davie still had some in a box at Cambridge.

The Sunday traffic was easy. He crossed King's Road and started up The Vale. The Vale—so many of the names round here echoed a memory of the lost countryside. The Vale then Mulberry Walk, and still with one mulberry tree in it Once there had been an orchard of mulberry trees here for the support of the English silk trade. All gone. There used until quite recently to be a mulberry tree at the side of the public library. They had cut it down when the new College of Science and Technology was built. That went without saying. "They" always did cut things down if they possibly could. Naturally.

At the cross roads Elm Park Road lay left and right. He turned to the left. Judging from the bells at the side of each front door the houses were mostly let out in bed-sitters. Nearly all the curtains were drawn. It was twelve o'clock on a glorious Sunday morning. The Chelsea bachelors were all abed.

The front door of Andrew's house was ajar. Davie rang the bell marked Wynne and walked in. On the door of the ground floor flat he knocked lightly. There was no answer. He was about to knock again when the front door opened. Silhouetted against the sunlight was a young man in blue jeans and an open-necked shirt.

"Are you looking for Andrew?" he said.

"Yes."

"Well, I've got a key. I'll let you in. It's all right. I'm a friend of his. My name's Jacko, by the way."

"Mine," said Davie, "is Davie."

"He was all out yesterday after a late night on Friday," said Jacko. "Is he expecting you?"

"Yes. I've an appointment with him for twelve o'clock."

"Then let's wake the wretch up."

But that was an unnecessary undertaking. The door between the sitting room and Andrew's bedroom was open. The bed was disturbed and Andrew was not there.

"The wretch is out," said Jacko, pausing on the threshold of the bedroom. "Chasing after the milk, I expect, or the Sunday papers. Do sit down. He won't be long."

Jacko strolled over to the gramophone and hunted in a box of records. "This should encourage us," he said. "This is the stuff Andrew likes."

To Davie's surprise he found himself listening to the great last scene of *Otello*. He looked round the room. It was neat and pleasantly furnished. The records were properly housed in record cases, not lying in glissading heaps on the floor. A full bookcase stretched the length of one wall.

"I think I know where he may be," said Jacko. "Half a minute while I run round to the Roebuck. He may be having one."

Left alone, Davie examined the room more exactly. Following the habit of a lifetime, he scanned the bookshelves. No poetry, some novels, some plays, many biographies and books of travel. There was a whole shelf of books about music and composers. There were several technical books about recording. A tape recorder stood beside the record player.

Davie sat down again. On a round table at his elbow was a piece of paper—a list of some sort. Davie was as honourable as most people, but, like most people, he suffered from an unbearable curiosity about odd bits of paper. He would not, under any temptation, have read somebody else's letters, but a list—Davie picked it up. It contained six addresses, and for a moment he thought he had seen it before. He soon realized he had not: he could not have forgotten the Reverend Samuel Corke, Mr. Miffin, Mr. Tuffy, The Reverend James Mugg, The Reverend Arthur Grumble, and Miss Ellen Masterbridge.

Davie sat back in his chair and tried to picture this exceptional sextet. The names reminded him of all the things he liked least—linoleum, antimacassars, heavy lace curtains, shut windows, aspidistras and evangelism. Miss Masterbridge, he felt sure, had dedicated her existence to interfering in the affairs of young virgins. Mr. Miffin was a church warden; Mr. Tuffy was the honorary secretary of some good cause; Mr. Mugg and Mr. Grumble were fanatics—Protestant fanatics: but Mr. Corke . . . ? Davie decided that Mr. Corke wore a biretta and was seriously concerned with copes and chasubles. It was a puzzle. What on earth would Andrew Wynne be doing with the Reverend Samuel Corke?

Unless—and yet the *people* . . . They were all the wrong people. Or they ought to be. Davie felt suddenly excited. He got up and wandered round the room again, peering impatiently at ornaments on the mantelpiece, at the titles of stray books.

By the bedroom door he paused. This was a smaller, darker room; darker at this time of day, though probably it got the early morning sun. Like the other room it was tidy, spoiled only by the confusion of an unmade bed, the linen and blankets of which were mainly on the floor on one side of the divan.

Davie walked back to the window and looked out. There was no one in the street. Then he turned back to the bedroom and this time he went inside.

On the top of the chest of drawers in a leather frame was a laughing photograph of Jacko on a horse. In another frame was the picture of a pretty middle-aged woman: probably Andrew's mother, thought Davie.

On the wall on the other side of the room, the side where the bedclothes lay spilled on the floor, was a painting. Davie crossed the room to examine it. It was a brightly coloured picture of some Italian village. In the corner he read A.W. Andrew was evidently a gifted young man. Davie conceived the idea that he wasn't putting his talents to the best uses, or probably that he had too many of them. But certainly, there was no doubt about it, it was a good painting.

As he stood there looking at the picture he heard the front door open, and "Not a sign of him," said Jacko, bursting into the room. "The wretch has disappeared."

It was then as he turned to face him that Davie saw the bedclothes from a different angle and saw something else there that checked his breathing. On the floor, protruding from the rumpled sheets, lay a hand.

"Please stop that music," said Davie quickly. And then, in the sudden silence, he said, "You must take a grip on yourself, Jacko. Andrew didn't go out. He's here."

Two hours later Davie was talking to Mays.

"I notice you don't say anything about this boy's death," said Mays.

"I didn't mean to be brutal and unfeeling," said Davie. "I don't know what to say. This boy has been strangled. I don't want to theorize about it. Other people are doing that."

"They are."

"I would guess that it has nothing to do with the tapes. That it's coincidence. That's it's one of these sex crimes. It's not my business at all. But it does occur to me—and that's why I talk about it and not about the boy's death—that, quite apart from this tragedy, this young man may have got himself into some awkward position—may perhaps have been persuaded to take a part in the matter of these altered tapes. He was in on the making of the tapes. He was out late on Friday night. We can see from his books that he had a technical knowledge of recording. And that list of names could well be the list of people to whom the altered tapes had to be sent. It's vague—it's weak, I know it is—but it's worth examining. If there is anything in this mystery of the tapes, then now is the time to unwrap it. If that list means anything, then now is the time to discover who these people are."

Davie paused. He was afraid he was talking too much. But Mays said nothing.

"If this murder had had anything to do with the tapes and Brent," Davie went on, "there would have been a search of the boy's rooms, wouldn't there? That list wouldn't have been left on the table. I would say that if there is any serious belief in this tape theory then it's very important that there should be no fuss and as little publicity as possible. If there is a criminal X then X must not be allowed to think that Andrew gave anything away. Indeed, he might be allowed to think that the death had made things easier for him."

Davie held up his hands in apology.

"Please forgive my talking so much," he said. "These things well up in my mind and out they come."

"Don't apologize, Dr. Davie," said Mays. "Your talking is very helpful. It sets me thinking too. Now you do some listening, sir."

"Willingly."

"I am ready to agree with you that there is something very queer about that altered tape. The whole thing may be a mare's nest, but I agree we can't neglect it. If he was the person who made the altered tape, then I have to assume that he has despatched copies of this version of the English course to certain people. And, in that case, I am also ready to guess that the people on that list may be the persons concerned.

"Now, assume that all that is true and what do we get? A mystery tape, which has cost trouble and been made at great risk, is apparently being sent to six people who ought to be respectable, considering that three of them are clergymen. Is that sense? If they are respectable people what purpose would this dubious communication serve? But if the tape is capable of serving a purpose, then doesn't that imply that all six of them are *not* respectable? It seems a pretty dodgy assumption to me.

"There is only one way of finding an answer to this, Dr. Davie, and that is to go and see. Each of these people must be—scrutinized. I don't doubt that the local authorities can tell us all about them. But I shall also arrange for them to receive—visitors."

Mays paused to draw one of his faces. A big nose, shaggy eyebrows, a moustache, an eye-glass. Evidently he followed a set pattern. This time he added a long cigarette holder, a cigarette and a spiral of smoke. Then he said, "Would you go up and call on one of these people, Dr. Davie?"

"Me?"

"Yes—you're just the person. You're not connected with the police. You can be what you are, a scholar. Interested in the church perhaps."

Davie considered, but he knew what answer he was going to make.

"Very well. If you wish it. It had better be one of the clergymen."

"Yes."

"But perhaps I ought to look them up in Crockford and see if I can find out anything about them."

"You ought to go this evening, sir."

"So soon?"

"An early call shortly after post time is what's needed."

"Very well. As you wish."

"How you work it I leave entirely to you, Dr. Davie. Which is it to be?"

Davie got up. "I incline," he said, "towards the Reverend Samual Corke. I like his name and he's the nearest. But I must consult Crockford. I'll telephone you."

For a moment he stood quite still. Then, "I am deeply distressed about that boy," he said. "I dedicate this investigation to him. In an odd sort of way it could be a kind of revenge."

Three hours later Davie telephoned to Mays from his room at the Gainsborough.

"You've made your choice, sir?"

"Yes. I hold by the Reverend Samuel Corke of Birmingham. I hope the whole thing isn't a delusion. I suppose those six could just be relations to whom he was prudently sending Easter cards. I don't want to joke about it—but the answer could be as flat as that."

"I don't think so, sir. That list was a carbon. You don't type idle lists and keep carbons of them."

"No."

"I expect you'll come back on the midday train. Please get in touch with me as soon as possible."

"Certainly I will. I take it that you are arranging similar calls on the other five persons on the list."

"Yes." Mays was not prepared to elaborate. "Good luck, Dr. Davie. See you tomorrow. And take care of yourself."

The telephone clicked. Davie collected his things together and walked down the stairs.

"I'm only going away for the night, Mr. Delgardo," he said. (Mr. Delgardo was on duty while Miss Mercer enjoyed the weekend hospitality of her Aunt Gladys at Southend.) "I'll be back tomorrow afternoon sometime. If anyone telephones or calls, you can tell them that much."

"Very good, Dr. Davie. I hope you liked your new wallpaper. Miss Mercer and I chose it on purpose."

"It is admirable," said Davie. "I like it very much. Goodbye."

"Goodbye, Dr. Davie. See you tommorrow, sir."

"Goodbye, Dr. Davie," said the aged Frank. "I hope it will keep fine for your holiday, sir."

"Not much holiday about it, Frank. I shall be back before you can say knife."

And so here he was in an empty first-class carriage, back to the engine, on his way to Birmingham, a notebook on his knee, and on the seat beside him a copy of *Emma*. Jane Austen, he had thought, might exercise a soothing influence against the agitations of the past week and the anxieties of the present one.

But first he must do his homework. He opened his notebook, and began to write.

The Tapes

(a) These scripts were composed by Marchant and directed by Miss Cragg.

(b) Miss Cragg was assisted by George Tallent and by two performers—one a college student, the other an actor brought in for the purpose. The actor, Andrew Wynne, was recommended by Marchant.

(c) Someone alters the end of the tape according to a pre-arranged, and very simple, code, and makes six copies. Probably six copies. There were six "slave" machines. To make twelve would have taken twice as long.

(d) It seems possible that Andrew Wynne did this and that he despatched the copies according to instructions to six people, who may be the six people on the list found in his room.

(e) The questions are therefore: who are these people? Why have they received this apparent invitation to a particular meeting? will they come? and who is responsible for the instructions?

(f) If the thought makes any possible sense that the tapes and Brent's death are connected—then it does necessarily mean that someone at Chesterfield is concerned with this code and understands its meaning.

Davie drew a line and began again.

Brent

(a) At present only obvious suspects are Werner and Robbin. Robbin because he has disappeared. Werner because he is an aggrieved husband. Neither reason seems good enough to me.

(b) If the murder has got anything to do with the tapes (and this is only a guess of mine, supported by no evidence at all) the question is—who was upstairs between about twelve-twenty and twelve-forty-five? How can one say? I know from my own eyes that Dyke, Marchant, and Blonde were there. And doubtless Ambrose was in his office. Of those, Marchant went out at three o'clock; Blonde at one; Dyke was still there when I left, much later; and Ambrose would not have left before five.

(c) Dozens of people could conceivably have killed Brent that afternoon, but only a very few could have heard the tape. If there is anything in the theory, and if Dyke, Blonde, Marchant and Ambrose are not likely people—then there must have been others, or an other, upstairs as yet unidentified. But who *is* likely?

(d) This seems to have got nowhere at all.

Davie shut his biro inside his notebook and looked out of the window. March was behaving in a very lamb-like manner. Soon it would be April. Was March 29 going to reveal anything? He had managed to find a copy of *Opera* at the Athenaeum. He had not been wrong. It contained no mention of the production at St. Botolph's Hall. But that made no mystery. There must be some other point of reference. Perhaps it would be *The Times* after all. The Pro-Opera venture would get a line somewhere. And what would it matter if the reference turned out to be something more secret? If he had made an accidental short cut to the right answer the true reference was only of academic interest. Davie looked at his watch. It was his particular time of day. He could feel his eyelids deliciously drooping. "Only of academic interest," he repeated and then he suddenly remembered where he had seen *Opera* at the Chesterfield. "I didn't know he was interested," he thought, "but I suppose . . ."

It was about an hour later when he awoke to see from the windows what Adrian Ballsover would probably have called a "conurbation". The outskirts of a great city stretched towards its center in rank upon rank of mean identical streets of slate-roofed houses.

Birmingham.

8

I

Somebody many years ago had planted a macrocarpa hedge between Potter Road and the vicarage garden. *Cupressus Macrocarpa* is a tree. Plant it too far apart and it doesn't make a hedge. Plant it close and every fifth tree dies, and the rest go brown at the base and thin. The macrocarpa hedge, if ever it makes a hedge, is a prime horticultural mistake which hundreds of gardeners continue to make in spite of the appalling warnings which neighbouring gardens afford. Somehow they always suppose—how vainly!—that *their* hedge will be different. The hedge that skirted Potter Road was not different. It was a shaggy, half-brown abomination.

"Ugliest of trees," Davie murmured, "the macrocarpa now
Is hung with rust along the bough,
All along the garden side,
Wearing brown for Eastertide."

At the gate he hesitated. It bore four very ancient and chipped injunctions—"No Hawkers", "No Circulars", "Shut the Gate" and "Beward of the Dog". Hawkers? Hawkers were a forgotten race. And as for the dog, Davie did not believe there was one, or if there were, he was probably an ancient spaniel with great floppy ears, amiably disposed to master and burglar alike.

He opened the gate and walked in.

Once there had been a garden here. There were beds full of rose bushes. But the bushes were unpruned and the grass was a foot high. There were daffodils blossoming unbidden in a corner. There was a thickly crammed border of irises. In its way it was beautiful, and mysterious as an early poem by Tennyson.

At the end of a broken asphalt path stood the vicarage, 19th century ecclesiastical in style and flaunting the horrible decoration of domestic stained glass, not only in the panels of the front door, but as a framework to the gothic windows. What was presumably the downstairs lavatory was so adorned that it looked like the window of a private oratory. Around the porch grew a huge wisteria. In a few weeks it would be what Mrs. Tibbs called a picture.

Davie looked at his watch. It was nine-thirty. He hoped he was not too late, but he hardly thought he could have come earlier. Beside the door was a large ecclesiastical cast iron bell-pull. He gave it a tug. There was no answering ring, and the thing felt loose in his hand. But there was a knocker. He knocked.

He did not have to wait long. Shuffling steps approached the door. Then a key turned and a bolt was drawn, and a chain rattled against the woodwork. The door opened.

The Reverend Samuel Corke was short and thin and rosy, which went well with his hair which was thick and white as snow and topped by a purple velvet skullcap. He looked at least eighty.

"Ah!" said Mr. Corke. "I dare say I am very late, but then you are very early."

"I'm afraid I am," said Davie. "I apologize."

"On Mondays," said Mr. Corke, "I do not have an early service. There wouldn't be anyone there if I did, you know. Come in. One moment while I collect the post."

He opened a large wire basket on the back of the door and removed first a copy of *The Times*, then a number of letters and circulars, and finally a small flat square parcel. On a white label Davie caught a glimpse of a sharply defined London postmark.

For a moment (so it seemed to Davie) the Reverend Samuel Corke hesitated. Then, with his back to Davie, he laid the small parcel on the hall chest and placed *The Times* on top of it. The letters he took with him to the door on the left of the hall. "Come in," said Mr. Corke, leading the way into a book lined room. "Pray be seated—but where? you rightly ask. Perhaps here. Or there. No—here I think."

Mr. Corke lifted a folio from an armchair and laid it on the floor. All the other chairs and much of the floor space was occupied by books, and the large writing table was covered with papers.

"So," he said, seating himself at his table, "you have found your way. If you had been a hawker or if you had been distributing circulars I am sure you would not have come in. You would naturally have been dissuaded by the notices on the gate."

"Nor," said Davie, smiling, "would I have come in if I had been frightened of the dog."

"Would you not?" said Mr. Corke. "Do you hear what the gentleman says, Hamlet?"

From the far side of the room came a creaking sound as of a basket disturbed, and then very slowly above the edge of the vicar's table arose the grave features of a very large Great Dane.

"Go and say good morning to the gentleman, Hamlet," said Mr. Corke. "He is not afraid of you, which will be a pleasant change."

Hamlet walked delicately round the table and took a long straight look at Davie. Then he lifted an enormous paw and laid it on his shoulder.

"Good morning, Hamlet," said Davie. "You are a very fine fellow."

"People who are afraid excrete adrenalin," said Mr. Corke. "And adrenalin communicates the fear to the animal. So the more afraid you are of animals the more likely you are to excite them."

Davie, who was in fact exceedingly afraid of large dogs, secretly savoured the air around him. He felt sure that he must have excreted a great deal of adrenalin but the only smell he could indentify was the overpowering smell of old tobacco. So Davie lifed a hand and patted Hamlet on the flank, and Hamlet, apparently satisfied by this courtesy, withdrew his paw and solemnly returned to his basket.

"People are generally very afraid of Hamlet," said Mr. Corke. "But he is a good animal and very fond of coming to church. He comes a great deal."

Mr. Corke picked up a large sheet of paper and began to read it as though he had forgotten that Davie was there. But presently he said, "If it were not for cousins marrying each other do you know how many grandmothers and grandfathers you would find twenty generations back?"

"Yes," said Davie, "I do. I worked it out once. One million forty-eight thousand five hundred and seventy-six, isn't it?"

"You are quite right, sir."

"It makes rather nonsense of genealogies, doesn't it?"

"Not at all," said Mr. Corke. "We are only interested in what can be proved. Do you know that only four families can *prove* that they came over with the Conqueror? Malet, Gresley, Gifford and Marris."

"I have often wondered why people are so anxious to be connected with the conquest. Surely it would be more gratifying if your family had been here before William arrived?"

"There are a few families who imagine that a silly rhyme is sufficient proof of that, but Arden, Swinton and Berkeley are the only ones now that Sokespitch is finished. I was sorry about Sokespitch. It was a splendid name. A splendid name."

Hamlet stirred in his basket and gave a low growl. Mr.Corke looked out of the window. "Oh dear!" he said. "Here is Miss Athanogorus. Parish workers are very necessary people. The work of the church must be done. But they will come to see me. It is very inconsiderate."

From where he was sitting Davie had a view of the garden path. A woman of about forty was stepping briskly towards the door. Her hair was plastered on either side of her head like a Dutch doll's. As she passed the side window Davie caught a glimpse of her face. Thin-lipped and determined, he could imagine her inciting the Mothers' Union to unimagined extravagances.

"Excuse me," said Mr. Corke. "I must head her off; she would come in here if she could." And he shuffled off into the hall, only just in time, for the lady had opened the front door unbidden and had already entered the hall before the vicar had closed the study door.

For a couple of minutes Davie partly overheard a monologue from Miss Athanogorus which was half concerned with the flowers for Easter and half with one Bill Staggers, a choir boy, who had so far forgotten himself as to laugh at her while on the exercise of her parochial duties.

"Poor boy, poor boy," said the vicar. "I dare say he is easily amused. Think nothing of it, Miss Athanogorus, and yes, thank you, madonnas if you can get them and arums if you can't, though arums never seem to me to be flowers at all. Thank you, thank you, Miss Athanogorus. I am obliged to you. Good morning."

The front door banged.

"Bother Miss Athanogorus!" said Mr. Corke, re-entering the study. "She is so very much too enthusiastic." Then, reseating himself at his table and shuffling among his papers he said suddenly, "Abbot's Bunbury. Yes. I have looked over my files, Mr.—er—, and I am afraid that I do not seem to have collected anything at all on this matter. I am sorry."

Davie had discovered the nature of the vicar's absorbing passion by discreet enquiry on the previous evening. He had intended to make it the reason for his visit. But he had not expected to be expected. Abbot's Bunbury! He could feel the colour rising to his face.

It was Hamlet who resolved the situation by arising from his basket and stalking to the window, where he stood gazing down the garden for at least a quarter of a minute before a dark and jaunty character in a light grey suit appeared at the opening in the macrocarpa hedge. As he walked up the asphalt path he waved some magazines gaily towards the study window.

"Mr. Palermo," said Mr. Corke with a sigh. "You see how difficult it is for the work to proceed. They will come to see me. Mr. Palermo is regrettably interested in the Boys' Club, whatever that may be, and he brings me magazines, which I suppose is kindly meant, but truly I don't want them. Excuse me."

After a minute or two's breezy conversation in the hall Davie watched the retreating figure of Mr. Palermo as he strode down the garden path, and suddenly he felt that he could hardly protract his own visit any longer. Truly there was not the remotest excuse to stay, and so when Mr. Corke returned saying, "Oh dear, bother Mr. Palermo," Davie got up and said "I must be going, Mr. Corke. It was very kind of you to let me come."

"Not at all, not at all," said Mr. Corke. "I am always happy to meet a fellow genealogist. But how hard it is for us to work. People call, as you see. And then the flesh is weak. I try to put off reading *The Times*, but I shall now give in, and I dare say that will occupy me an hour, and then I must take Hamlet for a walk. Fortunately Mrs. Mutton keeps the house tidy and cooks Hamlet his dinner. And then one sleeps in the afternoon."

"One does," said Davie.

"So really if it wasn't for between five o'clock and midnight I don't know when the work of the parish would be accomplished. The first eight generations are easy, as I am sure you agree. It is before 1500 that we encounter our difficulties. Well, goodbye, Mr. Wellby. I have enjoyed seeing you."

"Goodbye, Vicar," said Davie.

The door closed behind him and there he was walking down the asphalt path back to Potter Road.

He would, he reflected, have three things to report when he got back to London. He had established that what certainly looked like a tape had been delivered to the Reverend Samuel Corke. He had ascertained that the Reverend Samuel Corke was an aged and amiable eccentric: though whether he was as amiable or as eccentric as he appeared to be might possibly be disputed.

Thirdly, Davie had noticed that when Mr. Corke possessed himself of

The Times he had not revealed any small square parcel. It looked as though Mr. Corke had removed his parcel during one of his two absences from the study.

At the garden gate Davie turned and looked towards the vicarage. The Reverend Samuel Corke had not returned immediately to his table. Partly concealed by the curtain, he was standing by the window, watching his visitor out of sight.

Davie negotiated the macrocarpa hedge, carefully shut the gate, and found himself face to face with a tall bony man who said, "Ah—I expect you can tell me, sir—is this St. Wilfred's vicarage?"

"Are you by any chance Mr. Wellby?" replied Davie, suddenly inspired.

"I am. How—?"

"I thought you might be. If I may say so, I doubt if you ought to visit our friend, Mr. Corke, today. He is not at all well."

"Oh dear, oh dear," said Mr. Wellby. "I am on my way through to Abbot's Bunbury and had shoped to consult him about a genealogy. But I shall be this way again in a month."

"He'll be in much better fiddle by then, I'm sure," said Davie.

"It will be just as easy. Just as easy. It can wait. After all it's waited three hundred and twenty years—so another four weeks won't matter, eh? I'm glad you warned me. There's a lot to do at Abbot's Bunbury and I shall be pleased to arrive earlier than I expected. I've several days work to do there. Goodbye, sir." And lifting his hat to display a bald and knobbly skull, Mr. Wellby turned on his heel and made off with long skeleton strides.

Davie watched him disappear along the inhospitable reaches of Potter Road. He had taken a risk. He knew that. But a call by Mr. Wellby might have been disastrous. In a month's time nothing would matter.

He set off towards the station. The only thing that puzzled him was that postmark. Why Highgate?

II

It was not only Davie who was interested in the activities of the Pro-Opera Society. Already the booking had been quite brisk. Among the patrons of the new society were Lady Meade-Fuller and Sir Matthew and Lady Werner, and an archbishop of some Eastern church who was on a mission to Lambeth, having chanced to pick a conversation with

John Aristides, the Society's elegant secretary, had positively promised to be present.

"But I do think," said Miss Bleak, "that *Opera* should have given us some support. I sent them an announcement a long time ago and there is nothing in the March number. It's too bad."

"Are you certain you sent it?" asked John Aristides.

"Absolutely certain," said Miss Bleak, waving long fingers above her typewriter in a gesture of affirmation. "I posted it myself."

"I asked because there's a letter addressed to *Opera* in this drawer."

"Oh *no!*" wailed Miss Bleak. "I *can't* believe it. It's not possible."

"Don't get in a state," said John Aristides. "At the committee meeting yesterday Lady Meade-Fuller promised to make her husband advertise in *The Telegraph*, and Lady Werner has promised that Sir Matthew will pay for *The Times*. So he should. He's got pots of money."

"What from?" asked Miss Bleak.

"Oil," said Mr. Aristides. "Or something like that."

"There isn't anything else like oil," said Miss Bleak.

"There'll be the usual bits in the theater back-chat columns," went on John Aristides, lighting a Turkish cigarette. "There will be an audience. The question at the moment is whether there will be a performance."

"Mr. Aristides! How can you say such things?"

"Well, the way Dora Doranto is going on anyone would think she was a famous singer."

"They've got to go on like that," said Miss Bleak sagely. "It gives them confidence."

"As the stage is twenty-five feet wide and only twelve deep, and has no flies, no wings, and no scene dock, we can hardly expect more than to get the characters safely on to it. Whether they will ever get off—"

"Really, Mr. Aristides," said Miss Bleak, "you're joking."

Mr. Aristides gave her a grave bow. "I am so glad," he said, "to be appreciated."

Miss Bleak was never quite sure how to take Mr. Aristides, but she gave him a knowing smile and said that she would get the last of the circulars off by the midday post.

"They're a fortnight late as it is," said Mr. Aristides. "But never mind. If we can get the Pro-Opera chorus on to that stage we shall have scored a great triumph of art over carpentry." He stubbed out his cigarette. "Or, come to think of it," he added, "it would be an even finer achievement if the stage collapsed. That would be extremely entertaining."

"Mr. Aristides!" said Miss Bleak, above the clatter of her typewriter, "Do go away!"

John Aristides looked at his watch and went away. He had a lunch appointment with the archbishop.

III

"There is a gentleman waiting for you in the lounge," said Miss Mercer. "He didn't give his name. He said he was an old friend."

"Oh dear!" said Davie. "I hope he is."

He crossed the hall.

It was Walter Robbin who came to meet him, and, "Thank goodness you've come," he said.

"My dear chap—I'm immensely glad to see *you* . . . I take it you do know what's been going on?"

"Yes—but only just."

"Come upstairs. This isn't the place to talk. I'll order some tea. You'd like some?"

"Enormously I would."

Five minutes later, after Jack had deposited the tea tray, Davie said, "It's you who need to be informed most. Well—briefly this is it. Some time during that afternoon when you left the Chesterfield, somewhat in a hurry according to old Craddock, Morris Brent was murdered. You disappear. Every other member of the club has been interviewed and cleared—except you. Naturally there's a hue and cry. The police have been looking for you for the past week. And here you suddenly are. Where have you been? Why haven't you turned up before?—and why," Davie added after a short pause, "did you go away?"

Robbin drank his tea deliberately, set down his cup, and leant back in his chair.

"Where have I been? In Norfolk. Why haven't I turned up before? Because I didn't know I was wanted. I don't read the papers. I don't listen to the news. I was staying in a small pub under another name. It's a peculiarity of mine. You know it is."

"Yes, fortunately, I do. But it won't exactly be a point in your favour at the present juncture."

"Why did I go away? This is the difficult one to answer."

Davie waited.

"I went away because I had the most awful quarrel with Brent."

"I didn't think you knew him."

"I knew him," said Robbin. "I knew him a lot too well."

He paused a moment, then, "Look here, Davie," he said suddenly, "I hadn't the slightest intention of doing it, I'd no idea even that I *had* done it—but it appears, from what I've seen in today's papers, that I killed him."

"You killed him?" echoed Davie almost in a whisper. "What are you saying?"

Robbin looked at Davie bewildered. "I don't understand you—he's dead, isn't he?"

"Yes."

"Then I repeat—I killed him. I want you to advise me what to say when I go to the police."

"There's only one sane advice—tell them everything."

"You don't understand the circumstances."

"Then tell me."

"That's why I've come to you first. It's dreadfully hard to know how to put it."

"Just let it come out."

"You know Brent had been a policeman."

"Yes."

"I'd known him long ago—at school, just before the war. He was the school bully, the school beauty and the school hero. He was two years older than I was, and two years, at that age, is a lot older. When I got to the place he and a chap called Phillipson were running a protection racket. All the little boys were ordered to pay sixpence a week in return for which Phillipson and Brent were supposed to protect them—though what from nobody ever knew. I was a simple child and refused to pay. It didn't seem to me to be necessary. I soon found out my mistake. Brent and Phillipson instructed their little hangers-on to make my life miserable by day and at night they used to amuse themselves punishing me with a belt for alleged misdemeanours. I don't think I'd have stuck it if one of the prefects hadn't found out. He reported the matter. Phillipson went. Brent miraculously stayed.

"After a year the whole thing was forgotten, and Brent was as power-ful as ever. He was a superbly handsome boy, not bad at his books, a good cricketer and a great footballer. Nobody thought of opposing him in anything. There was no more protection racket. No more secret bullying.

It wasn't necessary. Brent was a king. And in memory of a past failure he used to beat me as often as he could think of an excuse.

"And then the day came when *I* grew up. I was sixteen and he was eighteen. It was the summer term and he was due to leave in a week. I was determined that he shouldn't leave school with nothing but the memory of greatness. So I and two or three friends organized a rebellion. On the last night of term, as he came back late from a farewell supper with the headmaster, we were waiting for him in the studies. As he passed down the corridor we caught him fore and aft, and carried him off to the baths; and when I'd had the pleasure of giving him 'six of the best', as the phrase went, we chucked him in, clothes and all.

"It was the only time that he'd been punished in all his school life. He couldn't take it. The term was over, but he reported us. The headmaster and the housemaster both thought the world of Brent. They didn't think anything of me. I was expelled."

Robbin leant back in his chair and lit a cigarette.

"Later on," he said, "I heard he was bullying recruits in the army."

"Well?" said Davie, after a pause. "There must be some more to this story."

"Certainly there is. After being in the back of beyond for a long time—economizing—I come back to the Chesterfield—a place which has always meant happiness to me. And I find that Brent has become a member. His name should have been Bent of course. That's what he was. Naturally I'm overwhelmed by this discovery. After lunch I go out into the garden to think what I'm going to do about it. I didn't know that Brent had seen *me*. After about five minutes he follows me out there and has the damned impudence—perhaps you think I oughtn't to speak like that about a dead man—but I'm still shaking with rage—I repeat he has the damned impudence to say that he's not going to have his life ruined by my presence in the club, and that I will have to resign. *I! I* am to resign—or else. You know, R.V., I've never been a patient man."

"You haven't."

"I knocked him down. And then, since I couldn't think what else to do, I left the club. And then I decided to go to Norfolk to simmer down. As soon as I was able to look at the matter calmly, or moderately calmly, I realized that I'd ruined my own case. Brent would certainly report me to the committee, and I'd be booted out. But nothing could take away the satisfaction of having blacked that bastard's eye. After a bit I decided to come back and find out where I stand. In the train I pick up a paper and discover that I'm a wanted man. I also find that I've killed him. The paper doesn't know I've killed him; but I do. I'll go to the police at once, Davie— but how much do I tell them?"

"If you've only seen today's paper," said Davie, "perhaps you aren't aware of the medical evidence at the coroner's inquest."

"No."

"Brent didn't die from any blow. He was suffocated."

"*Suffocated*?"

Davie nodded. "After being knocked out."

"You mean accidentally suffocated?"

"I do not. I mean deliberately suffocated. I mean murdered."

"Then, I didn't kill him!" said Robbin, his whole face suddenly transformed.

"The question is," said Davie, "whether it can be proved that anyone else *did*. I think I'd better ring up Mays at Scotland Yard and tell him you're coming round."

"How much of that do I have to tell him?"

"Not all, at this stage. You had a quarrel. He insulted you. If you're asked what the quarrel was about, you can reserve the right not to answer."

"Thanks, Davie."

"I'll come too."

"That will be a great help."

"I won't go in with you—but I've got to see the big noise myself."

IV

At the house in Fitzroy Square Matthew Werner was talking to Lucy. "We have been absent from each other a whole week," he said. "And that's more than enough. I can't let this go on."

Lucy said nothing.

"I was jealous. Of course I was jealous. But everything's different now. It's been a great shock to both of us."

Still Lucy said nothing. She might have said she was sorry for her part in the estrangement. She might even have admitted to a fault. But that was not like Lucy. Matthew had suspected her. The fact that he had done so with fair cause was not the point as she saw it. Matthew should never have behaved like that. He had been angry, had threatened to leave her at the very moment when this horrible tragedy had frightened her and impinged upon her happiness and security. If Matthew was going to come back to her it had better be cap in hand. Certainly she wasn't going to take any unnecessary step towards him if there was a chance that he would take the necessary steps towards her. So she said, "Only tell me one thing, Matthew. Tell me that there was no 18th century nonsense about a man's honour and all that. Please tell me right out that you didn't kill Morris like some cheap suspicious husband in a historical novel."

"Lucy," he said—and waited some seconds so that he forced her to lift her head and look him in the eyes. "Lucy—you know I didn't behave like a cheap suspicious husband in a historical novel. Of course I didn't."

"I never thought you did, Matthew."

"I'm coming back, Lucy; we'll start again."

Lucy looked down at the carpet. It was not in her nature to resign an advantage. "All right, Matthew. But let me say one thing. Don't think I don't know about *your* goings-on."

"*My* goings-on!"

"Yes, Matthew—I know all about your little friend. I always have known."

"Now look here, Lucy—"

"Matthew! Don't let's quarrel. Not again. We'd far better stick together. We suit each other. And it's so expensive to quarrel. It's not worth it. Money's important, Matthew."

"Money's important!" Suddenly Matthew Werner roared with laughter. "Lucy, you are the most extraordinary girl. I adore you. Come here! 'Money's important'. No one in the world would have said that, at this moment, but you. It certainly is. And there's lots of it for you, my sweet."

"Matthew."

Afterwards, when Lucy was sitting at her dressing table redoing her makeup, she spoke of the Pro-Opera Society. "I expect it will be pretty dire," she said, "and maybe there'll be nobody there. Somehow or other it failed to get into *Opera.* At the committee meeting yesterday the alluring Mr. Aristides said you'd told him you'd pay for some ads in *The Times.*"

"Yes, I did," said Matthew in a far-away voice. He was lying flat on his face on top of Lucy's bed. Without looking around Lucy surveyed him in her looking glass. Certainly he was beautifully made and she loved the way his hair grew down to a point on the nape of his neck.

"I didn't want to be connected with a flop," Matthew added, rolling over on his back. Still Lucy looked at him. She must have been crazy, she thought. Morris Brent was nothing compared with Matthew.

"Of course I confirmed that," Lucy went on, picking up her lipstick, and filling the glass with her own attractive face. "And then Lady Meade-Fuller said she'd make her husband pay for *The Telegraph*."

"I suppose we'll have to go."

"Of course we will."

"It'll have to be the first night for me—the twenty-eighth."

"Very well. I'll book them."

The little gold clock, boldly displaying its naked mechanism on the mantelpiece, chimed seven. Lucy looked from it to Matthew and almost laughed.

"If we're going out to dinner," she said, "it's time you put some clothes on."

V

Mays listened to Davie's report in silence. Then, "You certainly did what you were asked to do, sir. What you say is all very interesting, very odd, and exactly to pattern." He picked up five pieces of paper and sorted them for a few seconds. "You will remember saying that you presumed the other persons on the list would be visited."

"Yes."

"They were—and the visitors have all reported to me by telephone. Nobody had quite the luck that you did, but one visitor was able to see a small square parcel being delivered to the house of Mr. Tuffy. I don't doubt all six of them received their communications."

"But why from Highgate?"

"I don't know that that's very remarkable. If people want to confuse the issue in a postal matter they often do go to an unusual-for-them post-office."

Davie nodded.

"More interesting than any postmark is the very strange result which emerges from the combined reports of the visitors."

"What you meant just now by the word 'pattern'?"

"Yes. Every one of these five persons, Dr. Davie, turns out to be either a good honest simple person devoted to the task of serving his fellow men, or else to be ancient, eccentric and withdrawn, like your Mr. Corke. Moreover—and this is something you seem to have skipped, Dr. Davie—

none of the five appears to be interested in tape recorders, or to be remotely acquainted with them . . . So?"

"That is very strange—but rather exhilarating, Inspector. Certain comments spring to the mind. I've no doubt you will have thought of them long ago."

"Go on."

"If this business should turn out to be something dangerous then it would be only natural that six consummate actors would be required for its prosecution."

"Weak," said Mays. "If it were one person—perhaps. Here are six. Six consummate actors."

"They are not expecting to be rumbled all at once," said Davie.

"No—that's true. Next?"

"If a tape recorder is to be a necessary instrument for carrying out a villainous undertaking then one may reasonably suppose that it would be kept well hidden. One might as well expect a spy to keep his transmitter on the dining room table."

"I agree."

"I purposely didn't mention tape recorders to Mr. Corke. I didn't want to expose the reason for my call. He was a very eccentric old man, but I wasn't entirely satisfied about his simple goodness. He did seem a bit dodgy about the parcel. But I don't want to exaggerate that. I could have been looking for things that weren't there. What do we do now?"

"We go forward. The thing is too mysterious to drop."

"I was proposing to take two seats for the performance at St. Botolph's Assembly Hall on the twenty-ninth. Will you accompany me, Inspector?"

"Thank you. I shall be delighted. But they better be back seats. We shan't be looking very much at the opera."

"I hadn't thought of that."

"We shall also be purchasing seats in the house for some of our men. They don't often have a chance of going to the opera. It will be a new experience for them."

"Pro-Opera will be overwhelmed by the extent of the booking."

The interview was plainly over, but "I hope you won't think me interfering," Davie added after an embarrassed pause, "but—you've seen Mr. Robbin?"

"Yes, Dr. Davie. He seemed straight."

"I promise you he is."

"But he's in an awkward position."

"He's free?"

"Oh yes. But under observation—naturally."

VI

Dr. Marchant was not in the best of moods that night. It was all because the cold lemon soufflé had been a partial failure. Mrs. Marchant knew very well that it was essential to keep stirring over ice until the thing began to stiffen—but she had been in a hurry and had hoped that the refrigerator would do her business for her. It had not: and Willy had been very unpleasant indeed about the strips of gelatine which were hanging about all over the place. It was quite nice really, Mrs. Marchant thought, if you avoided the gelatine, but Willy had described it as a disgusting mess—and that in spite of the Pollo alla Romana, which was one of his favourites and had been particularly good.

So there they were, unspeaking, on either side of the glowing electric logs, which were emitting no heat because there was more than enough coming from the radiators.

Elsie Marchant was darning Willy's socks. Willy was looking at his letters. The girls, who avoided their father as much as they could, were watching television in the Den, as they whimsically denominated the room which had been allowed for their private use, in the first instance more to please their father than to please them, but which they now regarded as a city of refuge.

"On the twenty-ninth," said Willy, "I shall be home late. I am going to a production by a new opera society. I won't be to get a proper meal before I go, so please have a decent supper awaiting my return. Now don't forget. Write it down."

"All right, Willy."

"Do it now. You'll forget if you don't as you did that night when I came back from Covent Garden and found absolutely nothing."

"Oh, Willy!" said Elsie Marchant. "You know we thought you were at a club dinner. It was a mistake." But she got up and went over to her bureau and wrote something down in her diary.

"Are you going alone?" she asked.

"Going where?"

"To this opera."

"Yes—you wouldn't care for it."

"I thought perhaps Josephine."

"Oh no, no, no. Not suitable for Josephine at all. Look out for *The Tales of Hoffman*. She'd like that, I expect. Now I must get on with these letters."

"I don't think you ought to work so hard, Willy. You have no home life. You ought to deal with ministry letters at the office or not at all."

It was not often that Elsie Marchant expressed herself as clearly as this.

"These don't happen to be ministry letters," snapped Willy. "If the only business I did was connected with the Ministry of Education you wouldn't be living in this house I can tell you. Now do be quiet."

Elsie went on darning Willy's socks. About two years ago, she reflected, she had dropped the steamed lemon pudding on the floor while turning it out, and Willy had called her a clumsy cow. But he had apologized afterwards, and she had to remember that he had called her a genius when she made the crêpes Suzette so well in January. Willy had been in a particularly good mood that night. He had been making money, she thought, and she hoped it wasn't on horses. But perhaps horses didn't race in January. Willy never told her anything about money and really it didn't interest her at all as long as there was enough of it for the housekeeping and the girls. But she wished he wouldn't be so moody.

Elsie rolled the socks into three tidy balls, stuck her needle into a little green pad, and packed everything away into her needlework box. Then she went into the kitchen and put the kettle on. Willy liked a cup of tea at half past nine.

VII

Pink was Miss Mittens's favourite color and her bedroom in the very small flat in Beaufort Street was very pink indeed. The paint was "Magnolia", the paper was strewn with little pink daisies. There was a pink mat on the floor to liven up the grey hair carpet, and a pink bow on the dressing table, which was where she was sitting that night arranging her slumber cap in the looking glass before getting into bed.

Her head was still full of the tragedy at the Chesterfield Club and she couldn't get it out of her mind that she ought to play some greater part in the unravelling of it. After all, she, Christabelle Mittens, had been the only one to *see* Mr. Brent in the garden. Of course somebody else must have seen him too or he wouldn't have been killed. But nobody on the right side in this desperate business had seen him—nobody but herself and she did not think sufficient notice had been taken of her evidence. Indeed she sometimes felt that she hadn't really understood herself what she had seen. She went over it for the hundredth time in her mind.

"I went to the window and there he was, walking across to the gazebo. But I didn't stay because I didn't want to keep Madge waiting at the Academy. I remarked on the fact that a member was in the garden and Mr. Ambrose said it was too cold and then I asked if the Captain was next door and he said he was not and then I hurried off. As I went downstairs I saw the clock and it said eleven minutes to three. I can't confirm that because Craddock wasn't there and there wasn't anyone in the hall. I did see His Nibs going down the corridor to the telephones." (From motives of delicacy Miss Mittens always assumed that anyone going down that corridor was bound for the telephones.) "But he didn't see me—so that's no use."

"Well," said Miss Mittens to her looking glass. "I've done my best. I suppose I did tell the Inspector all that was really worth his knowing. But he didn't seem to *want* to know anything except the time when I'd seen Mr. Brent. He asked Craddock about people coming in and going out. He never asked *me*."

Miss Mittens settled herself into bed and prepared herself for half an hour's reading. But tonight she found it difficult to get on with *Mrs. Langtry: the True Story.* And when presently she laid it down she said out loud, "Perhaps I ought to have mentioned seeing His Nibs—though I don't really see what difference it could make."

The fact was that Miss Mittens could not relinquish the hope of playing a more central part in the Brent case.

"I've a good mind to ask Dr. Davie," she said as she put out the light.

9

I

Davie went early to the Chesterfield. He wanted to tabulate his thoughts. He believed he could do that best in the sober surroundings of the club library. He had begun this business by saying he was only interested in the mystery of the St. Martha's language tape. He was now convinced that the mystery of the tapes and the mystery of Morris Brent were inter-related. It was impossible to think of the two things separately.

If he were right in thinking that the playing of the tape in Brent's bed-room had been overheard, then everything depended on the people who were known to have been upstairs.

FREDERICK DYKE. What was there to be said about him? He was rich. He was secretive. He was a great, though unostentatious, opera-goer. This was vague and yet, at the same time, it was all to the point. He had been in the library at a quarter to three, and, according to him, he had stayed there till twenty-five to five, at which time Davie had seen him in the corridor. Matthew Werner had seen him in the library at about twenty-five to four. Dyke had no witness for the in-between times.

WILLY MARCHANT. He was the composer of the language course. He had recommended Andrew Wynne; and it was perhaps of interest that Andrew had been unwilling to come to the Chesterfield. Doubtless he didn't want to be heard talking about the recordings. Willy seemed to be rather better off than his educational office would account for: perhaps he had private means. And he went to the opera. Not as often as Dyke. But every now and then Davie saw him. He had been at *Rigoletto* in January. Usually he was alone. Either Mrs. Marchant disliked opera, or her husband dis-liked taking her. On the day of the murder Willy had been in to lunch and had gone out about three o'clock—a little after Robbin, Craddock had said.

There was more to note about Willy Marchant than Davie had expected.

BLONDE. Secretary of the club—he of the cold blue eyes. Davie thought a long time before writing anything down about him. He was well-to-do certainly. His furniture and pictures betrayed that much. But, except for one thing, the points about him seemed finicking. The spiral fire escape led from the garden to his room. Davie had thought he had seen footprints already on it when he and Blonde had used it that morning a week ago. But they might have been there for days, and anyhow the rain had washed them away.

Then Blonde had been against Brent's election to the club. Was that a point? It was a Blimpish view to hold, but understandable. On the other hand there could have been a more serious reason for disliking an ex-policeman in the club.

At which point Davie remembered that Willy Marchant had been opposed to Brent's election too. He added a line to his notes about Dr. Marchant.

But truly a fire escape and an opposition to Brent's election were weak points. There was only one really interesting point to be made about Captain Blonde, and that was the presence in his room of *Opera*. The club did not subscribe to *Opera*. As far as Davie knew, Blonde did not go to the opera. Davie thought about this for a while, and then admitted to himself that the explanation might merely be that the magazine had been left in the club, and had come up to the secretary's room with the other back issues. It was wonderfully easy to build up a theory on a prime misunderstanding.

Blonde had been out between one o'clock and a little after three-thirty.

The library door opened just sufficiently to admit the lean figure of Frederick Dyke. He raised his hand solemnly, but said not a word. It amused Davie to think that he had on his knee a brief analysis of Frederick Dyke. Certainly it had been wonderfully succinct. Nobody really knew anything about him. He lifted his own hand in silent reply.

Davie drew a heavy line on his paper. As usual, note making had helped to clear his mind. But it was not until he began thinking about Andrew that he received a flash of enlightenment.

When he had picked up that list of names in Andrew's room he had for a moment imagined that he had seen it before. Now, in one combined act of memory, he recalled *why* he had had that thought, and *where* he truly had seen the list, though without realizing it at the time. More than that, he could now understand where Andrew had got *his* list from. The whole thing was an accident. He never ought to have had the list at all. Andrew was entirely innocent.

He had been up half the night. Why not? He was young. He hadn't wanted to come to the Chesterfield. Naturally. He didn't want to run into

Willy. His rooms had harboured an essential clue—but with the business of altering the tapes and posting them away Andrew had had nothing to do at all. To Davie it was plain as a pikestaff that—

He got up abruptly, shoved his notes in his pocket and left the club. From the public telephone booth in Shepherd Market he rang up Miss Eggar. He wanted to know if anyone at St. Martha's was in the habit of weekending at High-gate.

"I haven't the least idea," said Miss Eggar. "Naturally the college is quiet at the weekend. If they have no commitments the staff are at liberty to go away, and they often do. Some of the students do too. Of course the students have to get leave. Not the staff. And some of the staff— Mr. Tallent for instance—aren't resident anyhow."

"Thanks very much," said Davie. "See you soon."

He rang off. As usual, Miss Eggar's information was clear and immediate, her curiosity firmly withheld.

Then he rang up Mays, but the Inspector was in conference.

As Davie stepped out of the telephone booth Miss Mittens went by on her way to the Chesterfield. Miss Mittens had in fact gone by some two minutes earlier, but, recognizing Dr. Davie at the telephone, she had succumbed to an earnest temptation, had retreated to the nearest shop window, and there assumed a deceitful interest in the goods until the moment when she saw Davie lay down the telephone receiver. Then, hastening daintily forwards as though a little late for her work, she had contrived to be in precisely the right place at the right moment. Davie raised his hat, and "Why! It's Dr. Davie," said Miss Mittens. Then, after a little ladylike hesitation, she added, "Excuse me, Dr. Davie, I had been wanting to ask you something. Could I have a word with you?"

II

Sitting in the writing room five minutes later Davie found himself chiefly surprised at the unexpected vulgarity of Miss Mittens. "His Nibs" she had said and then laughed at her naughtiness. And after all this conspiratorial behaviour what she had to tell him was nonsense. She had come downstairs and seen at a distance, down a not well lighted corridor, the back view of someone who was known not to be in the club at that time—Sir Matthew Werner. She didn't seem to have any reason for imparting this information, and it didn't point towards anything in particular.

She was just dragging it up in order to have something to talk about. Davie, like all the gentlemen of the Chesterfield Club, had always held Miss Mittens in high regard. Just now he thought her rather tiresome. A back view. At the end of a dark corridor. A smartly dressed man. And Miss Mittens did not always wear her glasses for distance.

Davie thrust his hand into his side pocket. He was looking for his handkerchief, but his fingers encountered a piece of paper. It was the throw-away announcing the Pro-Opera Society's venture. Reminded that he had not yet booked his seats, Davie got up and went down the corridor to the telephone.

It was John Aristides who answered. Davie told him what he wanted and asked how they were getting on.

"Very well, very well indeed."

"You weren't advertised in *Opera*. I thought it might have hampered you."

"That was an accident—but it doesn't seem to have hurt us. Indeed, we are selling rather well, and two of our patrons are helping us by paying for ads in the daily papers."

Davie glanced at the throw-away.

"I'm so glad," he said. "I'll send you the money."

"Dear old Mildred Meade-Fuller," thought Davie as he left the box. "Always ready to patronize the right things. What would we do without her?"

As he passed through the hall old Craddock was hobbling out of his cubbyhole, looking as though life could hold no further pleasures for him. "Drat it," the old man muttered and started to mount the stairs. He was off again hunting for a member wanted on the telephone. Truly the club's arrangements were archaic. There ought to be a page boy. It was absurd.

And at that moment an idea came into Davie's head which fused three thoughts together, two of them directly proceeding from Craddock, and a third which had only just been thrust on his attention. But of course! Craddock—Craddock—Craddock! The old fool was perhaps the key to the whole business.

Davie went straight out of the club and hailed a taxi. The thought that was racing round in his head was not for telephoning.

When Davie had finished telling Mays about "His Nibs," he recited his more certain conclusions about Andrew and the tapes.

"Well!" said Mays generously. "You are in form this morning, Dr. Davie. If we could put a tail on these characters on Friday and Saturday we might find if one of them has any occasion to visit Highgate. It might lead somewhere."

"That's what I hoped."

"By the way—that bit of tape which you found in the studio. It does contain the additional words and the music. Someone was careless. What's more important, it carries a fingerprint or a bit of one."

"I hope it's not mine," said Davie.

"That, added to your evidence, could clear this point completely. But of course, there's nothing criminal in making a tape and posting it to someone. There's nothing criminal in spending the weekend in Highgate. Absolutely nothing can be done about this yet: and absolutely nothing *must* be done about it yet, in case of raising an alarm."

"Poor Andrew!" said Davie. "I can't get him out of my head."

"I can tell you something which may comfort you a little," said Mays. "There was another attempted crime of the sort last night. It didn't come off. The intended victim was a judo expert. We've got the man. It's the same chap. His prints were in Andrew's rooms. That boy has helped us in two ways."

"I wish to God we could have helped *him*," said Davie.

10

I

When Davie reached St. Botolph's Assembly Hall on the evening of Wednesday, March 29, the entrance foyer was already crowded. There had been good reviews in the morning papers and opera collectors were in full cry. Here they all were, the old familiar faces—St. Pancras faces, Sadlers Wells faces, faces he'd been seeing for years. He knew a few of them to speak to, but for the most part they were just faces, growing a little fatter or thinner with the years. It was certainly a promising audience—but how many of them, he wondered, were police?

Plumb in the center, as though she were welcoming her guests at a private party, was Mildred Meade-Fuller, dressed, more for the district than the occasion, in a marmalade woollen suit and a necklace of enormous green beads.

"My dear R.V.—what a delightful surprise!" cried Lady Meade-Fuller. "This is too exciting. Do you know Mr. Aristides?—Dr. Davie. Mr. Aristides is the secretary of the Society, and he's been working so terribly hard."

Mr. Aristides bowed. He was wearing an exquisitely cut suit with a blue wild silk tie. Sapphire-looking links shone in his cuffs.

"I've often see you at Covent Garden," said Davie. "How did it go last night?"

"They all got on to the stage," said Mr. Aristides, "which, I assure you, was no mean feat. And no one was actually crushed to death in the harbour scene. I think we may modestly claim that the whole thing was a triumph of organization. My only anxiety is whether they will be prepared to take the risk a second time."

"It has always amazed me," said Davie, "that the people who built these halls never seem to have envisaged their being used for anything more demanding than a lantern lecture. Do you think they made their stages so small in a deliberate effort to exclude a theatrical exhibition?"

"If that was in their minds," said Mr. Aristides, "they have been out-witted by the Pro-Opera Society. The exhibition you are about to witness is, I assure you, unparalleled. I've never seen anything like it—

especially on the left hand side of the stage, audience left, during the big scene. Don't miss that whatever you do."

Mr. Aristides, in his own way, seemed rather good value.

"My dear!" Lady Meade-Fuller was saying, "how delightful! I'm told it went very well last night. You must meet Mr. Aristides, the secretary of the Society—Mrs. Mapleton-Morley."

Gently, with the skill of an old campaigner, Davie disengaged himself. He had no intention of being stuck with Mrs. Mapleton-Morley. And he wanted to examine the curiosities of St. Botolph's Assembly Hall.

Like many Edwardian public buildings, this was grand in a merely large way. The ceilings were high and from them depended enormous glass lanterns of a different period, added, perhaps in the nineteen-thirties, with a view to imparting a carnival spirit to the brown and grey marble pillars and the ecclesiastical arches.

On the wall of the entrance hall was a vast and romantically inaccurate picture of William the Conqueror receiving the homage of the denizens of Putney in 1067. On the staircase was a stained glass window with a jigsaw likeness of Edward the Confessor receiving the homage of the denizens of Putney at a still earlier date.

The hall itself was as high as a church and here—as a further contribution to frivolity—the lanterns that hung from the roof were constructed in a series of modernistic squares like a cluster of radiant packing cases. It was very remarkable, but because the electricity was all up in the sky the part of the hall designed for the seating of visitors was so gloomily illuminated that it was difficult to read a programme and impossible to enjoy the huge pictures on the walls, which showed the denizens of Putney doing homage to Henry I, Richard I, Henry IV, Queen Elizabeth, James I and Charles II. It seemed probable that only a lack of wall space had prevented a further demonstration of their continued fealty to George III, Queen Victoria and Edward VII.

Davie went to his seat at the back of the hall and looked about him. The room was filling rapidly, but, though he noticed several clergy in the audience, there was no sign of the Reverend Samuel Corke, nor in his heart did Davie really expect to see him. What emergency could entice that aged eccentric on so arduous an expedition? Six rows ahead of him he noticed the man with the red hair and the laugh like a saw. He went to everything. And there was that strange female antique with the extraordinary dyed hair. Davie had made a study of her for several years and had decided that this must be the only head of genuine hair which had

133

been successfully trained to look like a wig. And there was Mrs. Manciple and Miss Pannicker—Covent Garden figures. They did not usually venture into the jungle.

And then the lights were lowered. For Davie this was always a moment of delightful anticipation. But tonight he sensed a different excitement. In the half-light the friendly faces disappeared, and strange characters suddenly surrounded him. The girl in front, the tall man to the left, those others by the door—were they all hardy supporters of the opera? Or were they criminals? Or police?

To the right, about a third of the way down the hall, a door opened, and for a moment two latecomers stood hesitant in the light from the passage. Then Mays slipped into his place beside him. "Nobody's seen a thing so far," he said. "Have you?"

"I've just seen Dr. Marie Baendels," said Davie. But now the audience was welcoming the conductor and for Davie an ancient magic reasserted itself. It was years since he had heard *Manon Lescaut*. Within two minutes he had forgotten about the Reverend Samuel Corke. The Pro-Opera Society was putting up a very good show.

As soon as the curtain fell for the interval Mays and Davie left the hall by a door immediately behind them.

"I'll be in the entrance hall," said Mays. "If anyone spots somebody they'll stroll up and say so. But it looks like a frost to me. Dr. Baendels—"

"Is possibly a coincidence," said Davie.

"According to this morning's reports Messrs. Grumble, Tuffy and Mugg are in fact away from home. Why not the others if there's anything in it?"

"Do you think they might send substitutes?"

"No—the thing wouldn't be secret if it could be fiddled with."

"I think I'll go upstairs to the alleged refreshment room and have a look around."

"Do."

"I'll join you presently."

Another cluster of illuminated packing cases hung from the ceiling of the large and hideous room where a queue was slowly filing past a single dispenser of tea and coffee and biscuits, the only refreshments which St. Botolph was offering to his pilgrims.

"A deplorable sight, isn't it?" said a voice behind him. It was Mr. Aristides.

"Yes," said Davie. "Dreary in the extreme. But don't let us dwell on it.

I want to tell you how well I think the opera is going. The scenery's ingenious and simple, and the singing is far above what I expected."

Mr. Aristides looked honestly pleased. His elaborate ironical manner was not the whole of him.

"It truly is *the* most ghastly stage. The dressing rooms are appalling; the lighting is invented for the occasion; there's no bar; the refreshment room is a morgue; and there wouldn't even be a cloakroom if we hadn't fixed that up ourselves. Sorry. I've got to talk to that endearing little man over there. He's press and clamouring for news."

Davie walked downstairs to the entrance hall. On the last step he paused and from that small elevation surveyed the scene. The first thing he noticed was Richard Serpent drifting gradually towards the exit with an over-acted expression of preoccupation on his equine features. Serpent was well known for his apparent detestation of music—a great handicap in a music critic. It was customary to see him escaping before the last act.

In a far corner, taking good care to avoid any possible advances from anybody, was Frederick Dyke. In a costume film, thought Davie, one would identify him instantly as the man who was about to assassinate the Czar. On the other side of the hall Willy Marchant was in the throes of a conversation with Mrs. Mapleton-Morley, an ordeal happily endured (Davie guessed) for the sake of the achievement. Mrs. Mapleton-Morley was a good name for future quotation.

Mildred Meade-Fuller had gravitated naturally to the center of the arena, and was having a delightful time with the impressively bearded Eastern nuncio, Mr. Aristides's latest conquest. And there was Dr. Marie Baendels, accompanied by a man some years younger than herself. Her hair had been newly gilded, the dark parting banished. Looking up at the instant, she caught Davie's eye and waved a festive hand at him. Tonight her nails were emerald green and they flashed in the light of the lanterns like the claws of a vampire. It seemed appropriate that Jack Pincock should be standing just behind her, clearly meditating an atrabilious review for *Aria*.

Davie scanned the familiar faces with pleasure, and the unfamiliar faces with interest, and presently came upon a face that was neither one nor the other. He had not seen him often, that dark handsome Mediterranean-looking clergyman. But it was not a face to forget, and he had met it somewhere recently. It was, he thought, more a St. Pancras face than a Covent Garden face. But he couldn't decide where he had seen it, and he was still turning the question over in his mind when the bell began to ring. All the conversations mounted to a peak and suddenly subsided. Everyone turned towards the staircase.

Davie stood aside and waited for Mays.

"Anything?" he asked.

"Nothing. It's a frost."

"In that case let's attempt to enjoy the opera."

"Unfortunately I don't enjoy opera," said Mays, mounting the stairs. It was not difficult to perceive that the inspector was already embarrassed by the presence of plain clothes policemen eagerly awaiting the unmasking of a mare's nest.

Davie, taking things easily, was soon separated from Mays. Indeed he was last in the queue, except for the handsome clergyman, who hesitated a moment and then turned aside and walked down the corridor towards the cloak-rooms. And as he turned he offered Davie a view of his side face.

One foot on one stair, one on another, his hand on the banister, Davie stood suddenly still, watching the retreating figure of a man he had certainly seen recently, but who, very fortunately, had never seen *him*. Davie had seen him through the front window of Mr. Corke's library as he came up the garden path, jovially waving a bunch of magazines: he had seen him through the side window as he approached the front door: he had seen him going back towards the macrocarpa hedge. It was Mr. Palermo.

Mays had said there could not be a substitute. He was right. Mr. Palermo was no substitute. He was the man for whom the tape had been intended. Mr. Corke was an accommodation address. Mr. Tuffy, Mr. Grumble, Mr. Miffin, Mr. Mugg, and Miss Masterbridge, were all accommodation addresses. It was as plain as Jane.

Davie looked up the staircase. There was no one in sight. Distantly he could hear the subdued buzz of an audience awaiting the return of the conductor. He looked down the empty corridor, and he had no doubt about what he would have to do. To run after Mays would be useless. The only thing he could possibly do was to follow Mr. Palermo.

Quickly and quietly he set off along the corridor.

Immediately around the corner to the left was a door which led first to the makeshift cloakroom and, further on, the lavatories. The door was closed but not actually shut. Davie opened it boldly. It was no use creeping about. He must pretend to be on an errand similar to Mr. Palermo's.

The cloakroom was empty. Then Mr. Palermo must have gone on into the lavatories. Davie considered: if he did the same he would only inform Mr. Palermo of his presence. It would, he thought, be better to conceal himself in the cloakroom and see what happened. He lifted the flap in the counter, moved swiftly in and placed himself behind the second row of coat hangers. If anyone surprised him he could say he was looking for his hat. It would not be unreasonable. There was no attendant.

It was well timed. A few seconds later he heard the door to the lavatories swing open and back. Then soft footsteps walked swiftly past the cloakroom, and the door to the corridor creaked open. Davie began to fear he was making a fool of himself. If Mr. Palermo was out and away what was the good of insanely concealing himself among the overcoats? But Mr. Palermo—if it were Mr. Palermo—was not out and away. The door creaked back again. The soft footsteps returned. Presumably their owner had been taking a reassuring survey of an empty corridor. He lifted the counter flap. Stooping down and peering between two coats, Davie suddenly caught a glimpse of him. It was Mr. Palermo all right, and they were within two yards of each other. He was moving along the first rank of coats. Then he rounded the end of the row and started walking down the second rank. There was no retreat.

The mind is never wholly concentrated. The thought that flew into Dr. R. V. Davie's head at this moment of crisis concerned *The Boys' Own Paper*. How many stories in the dear dead past had he read about youthful heroes in exactly his present position, and how often had they been tickled by a cobweb and fallen a prey to that irresistible sneeze which betrayed them to the gun-runners, spies or pirates—thus providing the essential circumstances for the second part of the story, the escape. Davie had not the smallest desire to sneeze but he had an uncomfortable feeling that he was as certainly doomed to discovery as all those curly-headed youths who had starred in *The Secret Submarine* and *The Mystery of Castle Dangerous*. The only question now was how far Mr. Palermo would have to come before he found what he wanted. And then, suddenly, "Ah," grunted Mr. Palermo and came to a stop within two feet of where Davie was crouching.

He did not immediately put his coat on. With his back to Davie he explored the two deep pockets. First from one and then from the other he withdrew two parcels, in size and shape like half-pound packets of tea. Then he put them back again, eased himself into his coat, and turned towards the counter flap. But there he halted and Davie heard the spurt of a lighter and saw a wisp of smoke curl upwards above the line of coats. Mr. Palermo was not hurrying.

It was maddening. It did not matter in the least if they lost Mr. Palermo. Davie knew where to find him. But, if he were prevented from reaching Mays in time, five other people were going to get away without being identified. Unknowingly Mr. Palermo was playing a perfect hand. He had the only witness pinned to a spot.

For several seconds there was a cold silence. Davie was waiting for the sound of the counter flap. It did not come. And then Mr. Palermo's feet stirred on the tiled floor, and Davie suddenly realized that they were not turned away from him. Mr. Palermo was coming back along the first row of overcoats.

Peering between a mackintosh and a tweed coat (made, as he uselessly observed on the woven label, by Brown and Cameron, Inverness) Davie presently caught sight of him. He was going down the line of coats, pressing his hands against all the pockets in turn. Mr. Palermo was being curious; and in about forty-five seconds, thought Davie, his curiosity was going to be rewarded.

There did not seem to be any way out of this one.

II

Mays stirred uncomfortably on his hard chair. Dr. Davie had spoken of enjoying the opera. But the opera had been going for three minutes and Dr. Davie had not returned. As this made no sense May followed his wits (and his comfort) and very quietly slipped out of the auditorium. Supposing Dr. Davie had been right after all . . . For a few seconds he stood in the empty corridor. Then he made his way to the head of the stairs, and descended into the empty entrance hall. There was no one about anywhere. Finally he crossed to the outside door and opened it.

"Anyone gone out?" he asked the uniformed policeman outside the door.

"Not since the interval, sir."

Mays returned to the hall, glanced up the stairs, and then walked down the passage towards the cloakroom. "There must be," he might have quoted if he had read *Who's for Murder?*, "some explanation for the disappearance of Dr. Davie."

Then he pushed open the cloakroom door and found the explanation waiting for him.

Between two ranks of overcoats Dr. R. V. Davie, armed with an umbrella, and retreating backwards as fast as he could, was astonishingly defending himself against the violence of a furious clergyman.

Mays swung back the counter flap and dashed towards the end of the first row of coats. But as he turned the corner, aiming to grab the clergyman from behind, he caught his foot in the coat stand and staggered. The clergyman, reckoning the new enemy more dangerous than the first, had already whipped around like a spring, and now saw his advantage. "Mays!" shouted Davie, "Look out!" Suddenly in Mr. Palermo's hand there glittered an unclerkly knife. As Mays raised his arm across his face the steel flashed downwards.

It was then that Dr. Davie suddenly discovered in the umbrella an unimagined virtue as an instrument of assault. As Mr. Palermo lunged forwards Davie hooked him neatly round the neck with the crook. Nobody fights very well or very long with his head wrenched backwards in the grip of an umbrella handle. Mays, his hand bleeding from a glancing flick of the knife, had Mr. Palermo on the floor in no time.

III

"Dope," said Mays, three minutes later.

"I suspect," said Davie, "that there are five coats here which have similar presents in their pockets. If you can note the ticket numbers and have each person followed I expect you can nab the lot outside the hall without anyone else being any the wiser." And as Mays didn't seem to mind his babbling, he went on, "I wouldn't be surprised if more of them turned out to be 'clergymen'. I noticed several clerical collars in the audience."

"You know this opera," says Mays. "How long have we got?"

"About three quarters of an hour."

"Good."

"I'm sure you won't want to be bothered by me." said Davie. "So, if it's all the same to you, Inspector, I think I'll nip back and hear the last act. Agreed?"

Mays smiled gravely at him. "Certainly, Dr. Davie. Do that—but, if you'll excuse my saying so, you'd better unscrew your tie, and run a comb through your hair."

"Yes, indeed: thank you for telling me."

"The chap immediately across the gangway from your seat is a police officer. Please tell him to come down here at once."

"I will. I'll see you at the end, of course."

"Yes, please do, sir. And thank you for your help."

"Thank *me!* Thank *you*, Inspector. You couldn't have arrived at a better time if you'd been Jack Carruthers in *Castle Dangerous*."

"You certainly wield a very pretty umbrella handle," said Mays, returning the compliment.

On the staircase Davie ran into Mr. Aristides.

"Oh dear!" said Mr. Aristides. "What are you doing here? Not dissatisfied with our later efforts, I trust?"

"No, no," said Davie. "I had a call."

"A telephone call?"

"No, no, no—just a call."

"Ah," said Mr. Aristides. "Bad luck. But do get back or you'll miss the bit I told you about. Alas! I have to count the shekels. Audience left. Don't forget!"

Mr. Aristides tripped gaily downstairs. Looking over his shoulder, Davie was relieved to see him unlocking the box office door. The cloakroom, Davie knew, was not quite ready for visitors.

IV

Three quarters of an hour later, on the pavement outside the St. Botolph's Assembly Hall, the audience was dispersing. It is true that Jack Pincock was in the act of devising some sour remarks about the orchestral playing: the all-important triplets in Act 3 had been too slow and the delicate bit in Act 4 had been disastrously heavy. But, as yet uninformed of these defects, the general public had clearly enjoyed itself. The first production of the Pro-Opera Society had been a success.

"I do *not* understand the finances of opera," Lady Meade-Fuller was saying. "The Government pours out thousands of pounds in order to support *Cav.* and *Pag.* and *The Bartered Bride*—and then some society with no money at all puts on a wonderful production like this. All the really exciting things, these days, happen at places like St. Botolph's Assembly Hall—don't you agree, R.V.?"

"They certainly do," said Dr. Davie.

But he was looking down the road to where two men were accosting a clergyman as he was about to enter his car. Davie didn't think they were asking for transport, though it would have been only kind if the clergyman had offered it. At the request stop outside the hall an immense queue hopelessly awaited the coming of a No. 14 bus.

Davie spotted Mays and went to speak to him.

"How was it?" he asked.

"Perfect. They've all been offered lifts. Can I give you one, sir?"

"That would be very kind. Where are you aiming?"

"Highgate."

"Ah."

"We could drop you in Oxford Street."

"Thank you very much. That would be most helpful."

Mr. Aristides had waited by the doorway of the St. Botolph's Assembly Hall till the last member of the public had departed. Then he let himself into the box office and dialled a number. There was no reply. Then he dialled the Chesterfield Club. The aged porter said he would go and see, and after a long pause announced with some relish that the gentleman was not in. Then Mr. Aristides took a notebook from his pocket and looked up a third number. He hesitated before dialling this one. But presently he did so. A woman's voice answered him.

"Yes? Yes, it is. Yes. Yes. Who is it speaking? I'll see."

V

She had never wanted to have a telephone in the Highgate house. This Regency cottage with its adorably prim verandah was a secret place. The only other person who knew about it was the man who had given it to her, had furnished it, had chosen the curtains to match her eyes. The whole house reflected his taste, from the charming Monet which hung in the drawing-room, facing the window, to the entertaining pieces of Meissen and the pasture of Rockingham and Staffordshire cows in the alcoves on either side of the fireplace. Everything in the house had been given by him and he was the only person she wanted to see there. So why spoil it all with a beastly telephone? But that was the one thing on which he had opposed her. He might possibly need to use it. In certain circumstances it might be necessary for him to be rung up. And so the telephone had come, and occasionally she had used it. And she was bound to admit that it never rang, except once or twice on a wrong number. Almost it wasn't there, she used to think. Almost her secret house was a secret.

But now, tonight, it was ringing, ringing insistently. Clang-clang, clang-clang. She would have let the thing ring itself to a standstill, but he said, "Answer it," and so she reached across to the bedside table and lifted the ivory handpiece.

"Yes? Yes, it is. Yes. Yes. Who is it speaking? I'll see." She buried the earpiece in her pillow. "It's a Mr. Aristides," she said.

"Hand it over . . . Well? I said only in emergency."

She could hear the far-away voice saying, "This is an emergency."

She got out of bed, put on a wrap, and walked into the drawing-room. Partly she did not want to eavesdrop. Partly she did not want to know. "Emergency" was a horrible word. She had always expected something to destroy her happiness. She was frightened.

The curtains were not drawn across the windows and the china by the fireplace gleamed in the lamplight from the street. She stood by the side of the window and peered into the road. There was a man standing on the other side by the bus stop. It was late for a bus. Further down the road a car drew up to the pavement. Some men got out.

Then the telephone clicked, and presently she could hear him moving about in the next room. She would have liked him to come to her. As he did not, she went to him. He was dressing.

"You're not going?"

"You can see I am."

"I'm sorry. I didn't mean to be stupid. But why—"

"Because I'm in the devil of a hurry, my sweet. So don't delay me."

In the hall she took him in her arms. "Don't be away long," she whispered. "Don't be away long."

"Truly, I won't," he said. "But I must go now."

Then he kissed her hands, and opened the door.

Two men were waiting on the step.

"Sir Matthew Werner?" said Chief Inspector Mays. "Miss Mary Cragg?"

11

I

It was April, and Davie had come down to have lunch with Miss Eggar in fulfillment of his long promise to tell her all about it. The french windows were open in the drawing room. Outside, on the terrace, three of the four cats were assembled in the sunshine in their familiar abandoned attitudes. But Reginald's pleasure was to sit on Davie's lap.

"It's odd," said Davie, "how the explanation of a whole chain of events can proceed from just one clue. I would never have got anywhere with the Brauer tragedy if it hadn't been for that rose petal. And I'd never have made sense of this business if poor Andrew had kept his appointment with me that Sunday morning. If he'd been there I wouldn't have snooped that list of addresses. And he wouldn't have been able to tell me anything because he didn't know anything. I had even thought that he was the person who had altered the tape."

"I didn't," Miss Eggar. "I never thought that."

"But because he wasn't there I saw that list—and the list led me backwards to Mary Cragg, to Highgate, to Werner: and forwards to Mr. Corke, to Mr. Palermo, and back to Werner. Everything sprang from that list— and of course from your finding the tape at the back of the drawer."

"Elucidate," said Miss Eggar. "How did Andrew get hold of the list?"

"I think by accident. I remember he put his things down on Mary Cragg's untidy table while he drew me a plan of his whereabouts in Chelsea. I'm pretty sure he picked up the list when he gathered up his things again. When I found it in his room I felt that I'd seen it before—and I had. Mary Cragg dropped some papers and I picked them up. I was vaguely aware that one of the papers was a list of addresses. Later I realized that it must have been the top copy of the list I'd seen at Andrew's. And as soon as that became clear it was obvious that it must have been Mary Cragg who did the alteration—and, after all, who better placed than she? Afterwards the matter was clinched by her fingerprint, found on that bit of tape in the waste bin. It was the accident of the Highgate postmark that linked her with Werner. She'd posted the packet in Highgate.

Something must have taken her there. She was watched. Werner had a house there for her. She was doing this for him. She may not have known what she was involved in.

"Then I realized that Werner was paying for adverts in *The Times*. All of this linked him with the tape and the possibility that he'd heard Brent play it. Miss Mittens and Craddock supplied the rest of the information, though they didn't understand it themselves.

"Craddock had said that Werner had come down at one forty-five—and somehow the significance of the word hadn't seeped in. Down was downstairs. If he'd come downstairs he must have been upstairs. Brent had said he was terribly busy. I think Werner decided that he wasn't accepting that for an answer. I think he followed him, determined, I suppose, to have it out with him. I think that when he got to the door he heard the tape being played—went into the bathroom, and became convinced that here was a far more important cause of quarrel than the marital infidelity of Lady Werner.

"Then I realized that the aged Craddock was continually having to leave his cubbyhole to look for members wanted on the telephone. I think that Werner, who had gone out to chew the matter over, came back to the club in search of Brent at one of those moments when Craddock was away. Indeed he must have done—but he was seen by Miss Mittens. I think he went to the cloakroom—Miss Mittens said he was heading that way—heard a bit of the quarrel through a window—saw Robbin dash out, and then went himself to investigate. He realized that Fate had delivered Brent into his hands and he finished him off—and, Craddock still being away from his post, he walked out again. Then he went back to Berto's, where he'd had lunch, and enquired about a book. He didn't find it, probably because he had never lost it: but it gave him an extended alibi. Then in due course he returned to the club, and had the cunning to ask immediately for Brent. He was lucky, of course, but it was coolly done. Everyone thought of Werner as a possible suspect because of his wife, and therefore nobody thought of him as a possible suspect for a totally different reason."

"It's clear enough about the tapes—but the Brent case: that's circumstantial evidence, isn't it?"

"It is indeed. He can say Craddock was mistaken. He can say Miss Mittens was mistaken. He can even admit to being in the club at two-fifty, but claim to have gone out again to get his book. He did do precisely that: but not, I think, at once. They'll need more evidence than that.

I don't doubt that Werner killed Brent—but I do doubt very much if they'll get him."

"That's what I thought," said Miss Eggar.

"At which point," said Davie, "I would like to observe that it is not I who am investigating the Brent murder. I have been engaged on an inquiry which concerned St. Martha's: and I think that's been 'finalized'—as my fellow member of the Chesterfield, Adrian Ballsover, would say. They've pulled in six dope pedlars as a result. And, on that count, I think they've got Werner as well. We didn't do too badly. I'm sorry about Mary Cragg."

"The folly of loving!" said Miss Eggar.

There was a movement among the cats. The sun in its seeming passage across the sky had ungenerously placed itself in such a position that the branch of a tree was now casting a temporary shadow on that portion of the terrace where they had been taking their leisure. First Harold and then Dora transferred themselves to a warmer climate.

"Life," said Davie after a long pause, "is a continued process of finding things less and less funny. Little children laugh delightedly because one says 'Bo!' at them. Adolescents, especially in company, are in a perpetual state of giggles. It is only grown-up people who lose their laughter."

"Shades of the prison house," murmured Miss Eggar.

"I am rebuked," said Davie. "It has all been said before. I withdraw in shame."

"Not at all," Miss Eggar said. "I am not aware that Wordsworth said anything about humour. Or indeed that he had any. But why are you railing?"

"I find life sad," said Davie.

Reginald lifted his head and gazed at the gentleman as though surprised that anyone could find anything to criticize in this sun-warm, lap-warm existence. Then, after several loud purrs, he stretched out both his paws towards the sun and fell instantly asleep.

But now Xerxes, also aware of the unwelcome shade, awoke and conceived an immediate desire to perform his ablutions.

"Xerxes is a very splendid cat," said Davie. "I like tabbies."

Xerxes gave Davie one of his long stares, and lifted his leg over his shoulder.

"Which reminds me," said Davie. "I have two tickets for a cello recital tomorrow afternoon at the Festival Hall. It would give me great pleasure if you would accompany me."

APPENDIX

APPENDIX

A LETTER FROM

R. V. DAVIE TO GEORGE CANTELOUPE ON THE SUBJECT OF CREME BRULEE

My dear Canteloupe—You asked me for the recipe for crème brûlée: or rather employed a particularly discreditable ruse in order to extort it from me. Here it is.

Place the yolks of six eggs in a basin and beat them lightly with two ounces of caster sugar.

Place half a pint of double cream in a saucepan and bring it gently to boiling point. Remove it and pour it slowly over the eggs, stirring all together. Strain, return to the saucepan and reintroduce the saucepan to the heat. The custard must now be stirred until it thickens. If your hands are quick, your eyes sure, your touch exact, you can do this on direct but very low heat—but if the custard comes to the boil it is ruined. It is therefore safer to use a double saucepan, and even then the water in the lower half should not be boiling. It means a tiresome deal of standing and stirring. Because of this there are some devisers of cookery books—and quite grand ones too—who tell you to put the custard in a dish in a bain marie and bake it gently in the oven. This is a deplorable heresy. Doubtless you can make a very splendid baked custard from eggs and cream (a crème caramel is precisely that) but it will not approximate either in taste or texture to a crème brûlée, which should be thick but never firm.

When the cream has sufficiently thickened (and it will always be mobile) pour it into a dish to get cold. Then cover the cream with an even layer of caster sugar, about one tenth of an inch deep. Place the dish in a tray—the toaster is convenient because it is deep and has a handle—and pack it round with ice. If you have no ice, you must use cold water.

At this point you ought to apply to the surface of the pudding the sudden heat of a metal salamander: but, as this instrument is not normally to be found in the modern kitchen, you must place the tray under an already heated grill: and watch it. When the sugar melts and begins to go golden— which is very soon—take the dish away. The operation is so quick that, with the aid of the ice, the cream is not affected at all by this violent treatment. The moment the sugar cools it forms a sheet of golden ice over the cream and the deed is done. Be specially ware of keeping it under the grill too long. If the sugar becomes too dark it will also become too hard to bite—a disaster frequently encountered in a restaurant, but never in a college dining hall.

You can decorate the thing with a frill of whipped cream if you like. It looks pretty so, but enough is enough in my opinion.

That is my recipe, my dear Canteloupe. I trust it will not do you a mischief.

Yours sincerely
R. V. DAVIE

P.S. There are 18th century recipes for this confection—so the claim that it was invented by a 19th century chef of Trinity College, Cambridge is manifestly false: but I do think it was probably rediscovered by Trinity. Today all Oxford and Cambridge colleges made a speciality of this miraculous pudding, and brazenly claim it for their own.

Lightning Source UK Ltd.
Milton Keynes UK
UKOW06f1900051015

259920UK00015B/197/P

9 781906 288044